BOOK 7

DEATH'S SHADOW

✠ ✠ ✠

BY DARREN SHAN

LITTLE, BROWN AND COMPANY

New York   Boston

Little, Brown and Company

Hachette Book Group
237 Park Avenue, New York, NY 10017
Visit our Web site at www.lb-teens.com

Little, Brown and Company is a division of Hachette Book Group, Inc.
The Little, Brown name and logo are trademarks of Hachette Book Group, Inc.

First U.S. Edition: November 2008

First published in Great Britain by Collins in 2008

Shan, Darren.
  Death's Shadow / by Darren Shan. – 1st U.S. ed.
    p. cm. – (Demonata ; bk. 7)
  Summary: As Bec's relationship with Dervish improves, werewolves and demons attack and she sends Shark and Meera through a window to another universe to seek Beranabus, and soon all must face an even greater force of evil, the Shadow.
  ISBN 978-0-316-00381-0
  [1. Demonology–Fiction. 2. Magic--Fiction. 3. Werewolves–Fiction. 4. Horror stories.] I. Title.
  PZ7.S52823Ddm 2008
  [Fic]–dc22

2008016437

10 9 8 7 6 5 4 3 2

RRD-C

Printed in the United States of America

✠   ✠   ✠

For:

BAS — my full-time shadow

OBEs (Order of the Bloody Entrails) to:
court jester Sean Kenny — resting in fits of giggles!

Reaped grimly by:
Stella Paskins

Embalmed by:
Christopher Little & Co.

PART ONE

✠   ✠   ✠

A WHOLE NEW WORLD

SNAPSHOTS OF BERANABUS I

✠   ✠   ✠

BRIGITTA *was sixteen years old and about to get married. She had been promised to a prince since birth. He was handsome and kind, and she was looking forward to the wedding. She had dreams of bearing many fine warrior sons, becoming queen of a mighty empire, and living a long and happy life.*

But the prince had angered a powerful priestess. For revenge, she summoned a demon on the day of the wedding. The beast killed many of the guests and kidnapped Brigitta. She suffered terribly, but the demon didn't kill her. Instead, several months later, he sent her back to the prince — pregnant.

Brigitta was in shock, but the prince cared only about the shame this would bring upon his family. He called in a favor of King Minos and sent Brigitta to Crete on his fleet's fastest ship. Her mouth was bound and her face covered, so nobody could identify her.

At the island she was led into the infamous Labyrinth,

where her face and mouth were freed under cover of darkness. She was left to roam the twisting pathways of the maze, until the Minotaur found and killed her.

Like hundreds of other doomed victims, Brigitta tried to find a way out of the Labyrinth, but her quest was hopeless. She could hear the harsh breathing of the Minotaur echoing through the tunnels, and the scraping of his hooves along the dusty floor. She knew he was following her, watching, waiting, savoring her anguish and fear.

Brigitta was in the final stage of her pregnancy. She hoped the Minotaur would kill her before the baby was born, to spare the child a ghastly death. But she could not delay the birth forever. Eventually she had to lie down and, in the blood-stained dirt of the maze, deliver a squealing boy. There was no light, so she could not check if he was deformed. He felt like a normal baby, but she would never know for sure.

As she cradled her son to her breast, the Minotaur moved in for the kill. He did not mask his footsteps. The beast hoped she would run. He liked it when his prey ran. But Brigitta only sat there, hugging her baby and crying. Just before the monster reached her, she leaned over the infant and whispered, "Your name is Beranabus."

Then the Minotaur was upon her, and the corridors echoed with human screams and bullish howls of vicious delight.

✠ When he had sated his inhuman appetite, the Minotaur turned his attention to the baby. The child had been silent since the beast had separated him from his mother. The monster sat on Brigitta's severed head and picked up the baby, studying him with a vicious smile.

The Minotaur shook Beranabus wildly to make him cry. But instead the baby did something entirely unexpected — he giggled. Although he looked like a human child, he was a creature of two universes. He had the mind and curiosity of one much older.

The Minotaur growled and held the boy up by his foot. He clamped his jaws around Beranabus's head and squeezed softly. Again the baby laughed, then reached out with a trembling hand. The Minotaur thought the baby meant to slap him away. But Beranabus was only fascinated. He explored the beast's fangs and nose, patting and stroking them as if playing with a doll.

The Minotaur released the child's head and hoisted him up for a better look. The baby scratched the beast's scalp and horns. The Minotaur chuckled throatily, then winced as Beranabus tugged his hair. He reached sharply for the baby's hands. But although he wrapped his large, hairy fingers around the boy's pudgy wrist, the Minotaur didn't rip the fingers off or even bite them. There was something unusual about this baby that the Minotaur had never experienced before.

Beranabus wasn't afraid.

Everybody else had been terrified of the beast. His mother, the midwife, the people of his village. Even the godly Heracles shook with fright when he came to capture the Minotaur. Nobody saw the great hero's fear, but the Minotaur smelled it, and as always it drove him mad with hunger and lust. During his long years of captivity in the Labyrinth, *the Minotaur had encountered many prisoners sent by King Minos. Some were resigned and went to their deaths with a smile on their lips, praying for redemption. But they'd all trembled when the Minotaur breathed on the back of their neck and ran his claws along the soft skin of their stomach.*

But this baby was calm and confident. The Minotaur was a bloodthirsty, savage beast, but even at that young age Beranabus had a special way with animals.

Beranabus gurgled hungrily and tugged the Minotaur's mane again. Slowly the beast rose and smiled — it was the first tender, unhating smile of his life. He considered the problem of feeding the baby. He clawed through Brigitta's remains, but she was no use for milk as he had ripped her body apart. There was plenty of water in the Labyrinth, but the baby needed something more nourishing.

With another warm smile, the Minotaur stooped, held the boy in one hand, cupped the other, and collected a fistful of blood from one of the pools around his feet. With a gurgle of his own, he held his hand to the baby's mouth. Beranabus resisted for a moment, but despite his human form, he was of demonic stock. And so, with only the slightest reluctance, he opened his lips and let the Minotaur feed him, growing strong on the cooling blood of his butchered mother.

✠ *The next few years were the happiest of the Minotaur's miserable, slaughter-filled life. The baby was his sole companion, the only person he ever loved or who loved him back. He carried Beranabus high on his shoulders as he stalked the young men and women sent to him by King Minos. Some heard Beranabus laugh or coo as they fled and* wondered where the sound came from. But they never wondered for long.

Beranabus didn't see anything wrong in what they did. He knew nothing but this world of darkness and butchery. The people they killed meant nothing to him. They were creatures to chase, animals to feed on.

When Theseus finally came to the Labyrinth and, through trickery, felled the mighty Minotaur, Beranabus wept. Vain, proud Theseus was severing the Minotaur's head, to take as a trophy, when he heard the child's sobs. Startled, he followed the sounds to their source and examined Beranabus by the light of a torch he had smuggled into the maze.

Beranabus didn't look unnatural. Theseus thought the boy was six or seven years old and assumed he was one of Minos's unfortunate victims. He tried to lead the child out of the Labyrinth. "Don't cry," he muttered awkwardly. "The beast is dead. You're free now."

Beranabus glared at Theseus and his eyes blazed with a yellow, fiery light. Theseus quickly backed away. He hadn't been afraid of the Minotaur, arrogantly sure of his success. But this child unnerved him. The boy was an unexpected find, and Theseus wasn't sure what to make of him.

"Come with me now or I'll leave you," Theseus snapped.

Beranabus only snarled in reply and crawled across to the dead Minotaur. Theseus watched with disbelief as the boy spread himself over the monster's lifeless body and wept into the thick hairs of his bloodied, ruptured chest. Theseus stood uncertainly by the pair for a while and thought about hacking at the Minotaur's neck again, to claim his prize. But then he caught another glimpse of the boy's yellow eyes. It was ridiculous, but he had a notion that the child might prove more of a threat than the Minotaur.

"Stay here, then." Theseus pouted, turning his back on the boy, deciding to leave the Minotaur's head intact. If people questioned him afterwards, he would say the beast fought valiantly, so he'd decided to leave him whole as a mark of respect.

Following a trail of thread to safety, Theseus wound his way out of the Labyrinth to take his place among the legendary heroes of that time, alongside the likes of Heracles, Jason, and Achilles. He left the orphaned boy alone in the darkness, weeping over the corpse of the slain, demonic beast. He assumed the child would die in the shadows of the maze, unnoticed by the world. Life was cheap, and Theseus didn't think the boy would be any great loss.

The slayer of the Minotaur was a shallow, shortsighted man who cared only about his own reputation. He could never have guessed that Beranabus would outlive and outfight every legendary warrior of that golden age, and eventually prove himself to be the greatest hero of them all.

DEAD GIRLS TELL TALES

✛   ✛   ✛

ITS strange being alive again. This world is huge, complicated, terrifying. So many people and machines. You can travel anywhere and communicate in ways I never even dreamed of when I first lived. How are you supposed to find a place for yourself in a world this convoluted and uncaring?

Life was much simpler sixteen hundred years ago. Most people never traveled more than a few miles from the spot where they were born. Men sometimes went off to fight in distant countries and came back with tales of strangely dressed folk who spoke different languages and believed in frightful gods. But girls and women rarely saw such sights, unless they were kidnapped by rival warriors and carted off.

It was a peaceful time when I was born. No great wars. Food was plentiful. Laws were respected by most clans. We built huts, made our own clothes, farmed the land, herded tame animals, hunted the wild. We married young, bore lots of children, worshipped our gods, and died happily if we lived to be forty.

Then demons invaded. They attacked without mercy and dug up the remains of our dead, creating new beasts out of the rotting flesh and bones, turning our own ancestors against us. We fought as best we could, but for each one we killed, five more appeared. They terrorized villages across the land. It was only a matter of time before we all would suffer horrible, painful deaths.

In our darkest hour, an unlikely savior appeared. A gruff druid led a small band of our warriors on a mission to send the demons back to their foul universe. I went with them, and so did a simple boy known only as Bran.

We drove back the demons, but one of them — Lord Loss, a red-skinned demon master with eight arms and no heart — imprisoned me in a cave beneath the earth. I was shut off from the world of light. In the darkness, he sent his familiars to torture and kill me. The pain was unbearable and death, when it came, was a relief.

At least it *should* have been. But for some unknown reason, when my body perished, my soul remained trapped in the cave. There was to be no escape for me, even in death.

I was held captive for many long, depressing centuries. Mine was a world of darkness and absolute desolation. Lacking a body, I couldn't even sleep. I was conscious for every minute of every long day and night.

I couldn't see or learn anything of the human world, but I was at the focal point of what had once been a tunnel between the Demonata's universe and ours. By focusing hard, I could trace the shattered strands of the tunnel back to their source, and from there magically peer into the demons' den.

Not a lot happened in that part of the universe, but demons occasionally drifted by or stopped to test the tunnel in the hope that they might be able to rekindle it. I worried that one of them might succeed, so I kept a close watch.

After sixteen hundred years my worries proved well-founded. For the first time I sensed movement in the human world. A boy of great power had come to live in the area close to the cave. I could feel him being manipulated. He was led to the cave and tricked into trying to reopen the tunnel. I tried to warn the boy, to stop him. But he couldn't understand me. The tunnel was reactivated, and demons flooded through in the thousands.

That should have been the end, but the boy returned when all seemed lost. He came with another teenager and an elderly magician — *Bran*! My old friend had survived and grown more powerful than any of us could have imagined.

As strong as Bran and the boys were, it wasn't enough. Hundreds of demons stood between them and the cave. They tried to break through, but failed. It looked like everything was finished.

Then something remarkable happened. A magical force connected me with the boys. It united the three of us, and we became the Kah-Gash, an ancient weapon of incredible power. Without knowing what we were doing, we took the universes back through time, to the night when the tunnel was opened. Bran and the boys seized this fresh opportunity and put a stop to the onslaught, denying the demon hordes access to our world.

During the battle an innocent bystander — a boy called

Bill-E Spleen — was killed. I felt myself drawn to the dead boy. As my spirit seeped into his corpse, I found myself capable of restoring the body's functions. I set the heart beating, and it pumped blood through the veins and arteries. The brain sparked at my urging. Lungs rose and fell. Bill-E drew breath . . . and so did I. My first free breath after sixteen hundred years of imprisonment. No words can describe the deliciousness of that.

As Bran and the others stared at me, amazed and afraid, I set about altering the body I'd taken over, reshaping it, giving it my face, my build, my sex. Within hours it was a boy's body no longer, but a girl's, with breath, a heartbeat, bones, guts, flesh, blood, a face. I was *alive*!

That's when my problems really began.

LONELY NEW WORLD

✛ ✛ ✛

WHAT amazes me most about this modern world is that people aren't more amazed. I first lived in a time of magic, with priestesses and druids who could perform wondrous feats. But we had nothing like airplanes, computers, televisions, cars. We were servants of the natural world, ignorant of the ways of the universe and the origins of our planet. We didn't even know the Earth was round!

Today's people have mastered the land and seas, and even made inroads into the heavens — they can *fly*! There are things they can't control, like earthquakes and floods, but for the most part they've torn down trees, carved up the planet with roads, and made it theirs. They've hurt the Earth, and they don't seem as happy as people in my time were, but they've achieved the incredible.

I've been here more than six months, yet I still find a dozen things each day that make my jaw drop. Like a pencil. How do they put lead inside wood? And paper — nobody thinks twice about it, but in my previous life, if you wanted to record a message, you had to hammer notches out of a chunk of rock.

It's a terrifying world, and I shouldn't be able to cope with it. I came back to life as a small, scared, lonely girl. If I'd stepped out of the cave knowing nothing of what lay beyond, I'd have fainted with shock and gone on fainting every time I recovered and looked around.

But when I took over Bill-E Spleen's body, his memories became mine. It took me a few weeks to process everything, but I soon knew all that he did. That helped me make sense of this new world and deal with it. Without access to Bill-E's memories I wouldn't have known how to use a knife and fork, knot a pair of laces, open a door, or do any of the simple, everyday tasks that everyone else takes for granted.

But as helpful as that's been, it's also proved to be one of my biggest problems. Because I live with Bill-E's uncle, Dervish Grady, and I made the mistake of telling him about Bill-E's memories. As a result, he sees me as some kind of a medium, offering him unlimited access to his dead nephew's feelings and thoughts.

✠ "Tell me about Billy's first day at school."

We're in Dervish's study on the top floor of the house. The mansion is a three-story monster, full of round stained-glass windows, wooden floorboards, and bare stone walls. (Except in this study, which is lined with leather panels.) All of the people from my village could have lived in comfort here. When I first saw it, I thought it was a communal building.

"His first day at school?" I chew my lower lip, as though I have to think hard to retrieve the memories. Dervish watches me intently, hands crossed on the desk in front of him, eyes hard. I don't enjoy these sessions. He brings me up here three or four times a day and asks me about Bill-E, the things he experienced, the thoughts he had, the way he saw the world.

"He wasn't nervous," I begin. "He thought it was a big adventure. He loved putting on his uniform and packing his books and lunch. He kept checking the kitchen clock, even though he couldn't tell the time."

Dervish smiles. He always grins when I tell him an amusing little detail about his dead nephew. But he's not smiling at me — he's smiling to himself, as if sharing a joke with the absent Bill-E Spleen.

I tell Dervish more, talking him through the young boy's impressions of his teacher and classmates. I find this boring as well as uncomfortable. It's like having to read chapters from the same story, over and over. My attention wanders and my eyes dart round Dervish's study, the books of magic on the shelves, the weapons on the walls. I want to flick through the pages of those books and test some of the axes and swords. But there's never time for that.

Maybe Dervish doesn't see me. Perhaps to him I'm not a real person, just a mouthpiece for Bill-E. I doubt that he can imagine me doing anything other than talking about the boy I replaced. There's nothing malicious in it. I just don't think it's crossed his mind to regard me as an independent human being.

Eventually, two hours later, Dervish dismisses me. He's had enough for now. He waves me away, not bothering to even say goodnight. I leave him staring at his crossed hands, thoughts distant, a sad wreck of a man, more lost in the past than I ever was when captive in the cave.

✚ I love walking, exploring the countryside between the house and Carcery Vale. I like it in the forest. The land was covered in trees when I first lived. I almost feel like I'm in my original time when I leave the roads and paths of the modern world and stroll through woodland. Sometimes I'll pluck a leaf and set it on my tongue, to taste nature. I try to trick myself into believing the new world doesn't exist, that the natural balance has been restored.

Of course that's fantasy, and the sensation never lasts long. These trees have been carefully planted and the under-growth is nowhere near as dense as it was back then. There are still rabbits and foxes, but they're scarce. No wolves or bears. The smell of the modern world is thick in the air, a nasty, acidic stench. But if I use my imagination, I can be-lieve for a second or two that I'm in the forest near my rath.

Sometimes, in the night, I truly forget about the present. In my dreams I'm still Bec MacConn, learning the ways of magic from my teacher, Banba. I wake up in a cold sweat, heart racing, crouched close to the wall, wondering where I am, why there's a hole in the wall, and what the clear, hard material stretched across it is. I feel trapped, as if I'm back in the cave. I swipe my fists at imagined phantoms of this new, scary world.

The confusion always passes swiftly. After a minute or two I remember where and when I am. My fists unclench and my heart settles down. I find it hard to sleep again on such nights, and lie awake in the dark, often curled up on the floor in a corner, remembering those I knew, all long dead and decayed. I feel lost and alone on such nights, and tears often fall and soak my cheeks as I tremble and miserably hug myself.

But it's day now and I feel more relaxed. I move through the forest, humming a tune the world hasn't heard in more than a millennium, pretending that I'm back in my own time. I come to a bush of red berries. I'm reaching for a berry to examine it when I spot a car and realize I'm close to a road. I still feel uneasy around cars, even after six months. I haven't been in one yet, although I've been on Dervish's motorcycle a couple of times, when he took me to a nearby town to get clothes.

Cars frighten me. They look vicious. Growling, screeching, fast-moving assassins. I know they're not living, thinking creatures, but I can't help myself. Whenever I see a car, I expect it to race after me, chase me through the trees, and mow me down.

I wait for the noise of the engine to fade, then edge over to the road. I've explored all the area around Dervish's home and can pinpoint my position within half a minute, no matter where I am. One look at the road, the trees by its side, and the bend to my left, and I know I'm a five-minute walk from Carcery Vale, the nearest village.

I haven't been to the Vale often. The people there make me nervous. I keep quiet and don't interact with them. I feel out of place, afraid I'll say something to give myself away. I'm not truly part of this world and I can't shake the feeling that our neighbors will eventually unearth my secret.

My first week here was insane. We'd just saved the world

from a demon invasion, but there was no time to take pride in our achievement. Beranabus — as Bran now calls himself — left the day after our showdown with Lord Loss. We'd glimpsed the demon master's superior in the cave — a huge, mysterious, shadowy, powerful beast. Lord Loss said our hours were numbered, that we'd only delayed the day of reckoning.

Beranabus was overwhelmed by my reappearance. I was the only person he'd ever cared about, and my return brought happiness back into his life. But the ancient magician is practical above all else. He wanted to stay and spend his last few years by my side. But there were demons to fight and a world to save. There was no time for selfish pleasure.

He took his assistant, Kernel Fleck, and Grubbs Grady — another of Dervish's nephews — with him. Grubbs is very powerful, but he hates fighting demons. He'd spent his life hiding from his responsibilities, but Bill-E's death seemed to settle him on his path. As reluctant as he was to leave Dervish, as scared as he was to face the Demonata, he went anyway.

Beranabus should have taken me too. When Grubbs, Kernel, and I unite, we become the Kah-Gash. We have the power to destroy a whole universe. Beranabus should have kept us together, to experiment and use us.

He left me behind for two reasons. The first was personal. I'd suffered sixteen hundred years of imprisonment and he didn't want to thrust me into the demon's universe to fight immediately. He felt I deserved a few years of peace and wished to spare me the awfulness of my destiny as long as he could.

But he was scared as well, and that was the main reason. Beranabus had been searching for the Kah-Gash most of his life, hoping to destroy the Demonata with it. But he'd never been sure if he was chasing a mythical Holy Grail or an actual weapon. When he saw it in action, doubt crept in.

Was he right to put the pieces together? What if we fell into the hands of the Demonata and they used us to annihilate the human world? Or maybe the Kah-Gash would work against us by itself. We hadn't intentionally taken the universes back in time. The Kah-Gash did that, having manipulated Grubbs into helping the demons open the tunnel in the first place. It had a mind and unknowable will of its own. Perhaps it had saved us by accident.

Wary of the weapon, Beranabus split us up. He should have left Grubbs behind to comfort Dervish, and he would have if not for his love of me. Dervish went into a rage when he woke to be told Grubbs had slipped away in the middle of the night. Grubbs and Bill-E were his nephews, but they'd been like sons. Now he'd lost them both. He cursed Beranabus, the demons . . . and me. He blamed me for Bill-E's death, accused me of conspiring against the boy, tricking him so that I could take over his body.

It was the first day of my new life. Everything was confusion and uncertainty. I was awestruck, afraid, not sure what to say or how to act, delighted to be alive, but terrified. Unsure of myself, I let Dervish curse and scream. I didn't flinch when he jabbed a finger at me or lifted me off the ground and shook me hard, only prayed to the gods that he wouldn't kill me.

In the end he stormed off. He ignored me for days, and

would have ignored me for longer — maybe forever — if not for Meera Flame, one of his oldest friends. In the middle of his depression, he called her to tell her about his loss. Meera came to him immediately. After doing what she could to console Dervish, she asked if I needed anything, if I wanted to talk about what I'd been through.

Meera was wary of me. Like Dervish, she wondered if I'd led Bill-E to his death so that I could take control of his body. Through floods of tears I convinced her of my innocence. When she realized I was just a lonely girl, as scared of this new world as I was of demons, her heart warmed to me, and we were able to talk openly. I told her about my life, my centuries in the cave, the force that compelled me to take Bill-E's body.

"I didn't want to bring the corpse back to life and change it," I'd sobbed. "It just happened. It was lying there, good for nothing else, and I had the power to make it mine. In those first few minutes, I wasn't thinking about living again. I could see that Lord Loss was going to kill the others. I just wanted to help them."

Meera believed me and managed to convince Dervish of the truth. She also dealt with the difficulties of Bill-E's disappearance and my sudden existence. She got Dervish to pretend Bill-E had gone to live with relatives. Through her contacts, Meera faked the necessary paperwork and arranged for officials in high positions to throw their weight behind the lie if anyone (such as Bill-E's teachers) made inquiries.

Those same contacts forged a birth certificate and passport for me. I became an illegitimate niece of Dervish's, whose mother had recently passed away. In the absence of any other living relative, I'd been sent to Carcery Vale.

It was too coincidental to pass close scrutiny. A boy's grandparents are brutally slaughtered . . . the boy takes off without saying a word to anyone . . . his best friend also disappears . . . and a girl nobody has ever heard of moves in with the man who was like a father to both boys. The people of Carcery Vale aren't stupid. I'm sure they knew something was wrong.

But Meera and her allies covered their tracks artfully. Police were assured by their colleagues in other districts that Bill-E was safe and the girl's story was on the level. In the face of such carefully contrived evidence, our neighbors could do nothing except watch suspiciously and wait for the next bizarre Grady family twist.

FIRST CONTACT

✢   ✢   ✢

FROM the spot on the road in the forest, I make the five-minute walk to Carcery Vale but keep to the edge of the village, circling the houses and shops. I look on enviously at the ordinary people leading their ordinary lives.

Dervish is supposed to be tutoring me at home while I recover from the loss of my mother. Meera has supplied us with schoolbooks and equipment. Of course, Dervish hasn't once sat down to help me with schoolwork, but I've been doing it by myself. I complete the necessary exercises so that Meera can show them to the relevant authorities and keep them happy.

I enjoy the homework. I never did anything like this before. I learned how to do practical things in my rath, like cook, wash, and sharpen weapons. I memorized lots of stories, and Banba taught me magic. But I never studied books — they didn't exist then. I knew nothing about global history, geography, science, mathematics.

It's fascinating. I know a lot already, courtesy of Bill-E's memories, but I'm discovering much more. Like most people, Bill-E didn't retain all that he learned, so I only have access to the bits he remembered. But my own memory is perfect. I have total recall of anything I see, hear, or read. By devouring the books Meera gives me, and watching dozens of television documentaries and the news, I've pieced together many of the facts of this brave new world. Ironically, I probably know more about it than most of the children who are natives of this time.

I'd love to go to school and learn from real teachers. I study as best I can at home, do my homework, watch educational programs, and surf the Internet. But that's no substitute for being taught by another person. There's so much more I could do with my brain, so many things I could uncover about the world, if I only had someone to instruct me.

But I'm not ready to mix with other people yet. What would I say? How would I mingle and pass as one of their own? I'd have to guard my tongue, always afraid I'd say something that gave away my past. I have nothing in common with these folk. I know much about their ways from Bill-E and what I've read about them and seen on television. But in my time, girls married when they were fourteen. Warriors fought naked. Slavery was a fact of life. There was nothing odd about eating the heart of a defeated enemy. We worshipped many gods and believed they directly influenced our day-to-day lives.

As I brood about the gulf between me and these people, someone coughs behind me. I'm instantly on my guard — in my experience, if somebody sneaks up on you, they're almost certainly an enemy. Whirling, my lips move fast, working on a spell. There's virtually no magic in the air, so my powers are limited, but I can still work the odd spell or two. I won't be taken easily.

It's a girl. A couple of years older than me. We're dressed in similar clothes, but she wears hers more naturally. I haven't fully gotten the hang of shoes and laces, soft shirts and buttons. Her hair looks much neater than mine and she wears make-up.

"Hi," the girl says.

"Hello," I reply softly, putting a name to her face and letting the spell die on my lips. She's Reni Gossel, the sister of a boy Bill-E hated. Grubbs liked this girl. Bill-E did too, although he never said, because he didn't believe he could compete with his older, bigger, more confident friend.

"I'm Reni," she says.

"Yes." I think for a moment. "I'm Rebecca Kinga." That's the fake name Meera provided me with. "Bec for short."

Reni nods and comes closer, studying me. There's a hostile shade to her eyes that unnerves me. This girl has no reason to dislike me — we don't know each other — but I think she does anyway.

"You're Dervish Grady's niece," Reni says, circling me the way I was circling the village a few minutes before.

"That's right," I mutter, not turning, staring straight ahead, shivering slightly. This girl can't hurt me, but I'm afraid she might see through me.

"Grubbs never said anything about you."

"He didn't know. It was a secret."

"A Grady with a secret." She smiles crookedly. "Nothing new in that."

"What do you mean?" I frown.

"Dervish has always been full of secrets. Grubbs too. We were close, but I'm sure there were things he wasn't telling me, about his parents, his sister, Dervish." She stops in front of me. "Did you meet Grubbs?"

"Just once," I answer honestly.

"Strange how he moved out just as you moved in."

I shrug. "He was upset. When Bill-E's grandparents were killed, he wanted to get away from here. It reminded him of when his parents were murdered."

"Maybe," Reni sniffs. "But who did he go to?"

"His aunt."

Reni shakes her head. "Grubbs didn't like his aunt. Or any of his other relatives. He told me about them. Dervish was the only one he loved. Bill-E loved Dervish too. Yet both of them have gone without warning and neither has bothered to pay him a visit in all the months since. Like I said — *strange*."

Her eyes are hot with mistrust and anger. For reasons she maybe doesn't even know, she blames me for the disappearance of Grubbs and Bill-E. And to a certain extent she's right.

I say nothing, figuring silence is better than a lie. After a minute of quiet, Reni asks softly, "Do you have a number for Grubbs?"

"No, but I could probably ask Der —"

"Don't bother," she interrupts. "I asked already, when I couldn't get through on his cell. He said Grubbs didn't want to talk to anyone. He told me to e-mail, and I did, but it wasn't Grubbs who answered. I'm no fool. I could tell it was Dervish pretending to be his nephew."

I'm not sure how to respond.

"This has something to do with what happened to Loch," she whispers, and her expression changes, becoming more haunted. "You know who Loch was?"

"Your brother," I croak.

She nods. "Some people might say it wasn't coincidence that the pair who were with him the day he died have gone missing. Or that the grandparents of one were butchered. Or that the uncle of another has spent the last six months looking like a man who's lost everything — every*one* — dear to him."

"What do you want?" I ask stiffly.

"I want to know what happened," she snarls, and grabs both my arms, squeezing tightly. "Loch's death was awful, but I believed it was an accident, so I dealt with it. Now I have horrible, terrible doubts. There's more going on than anyone knows. Dervish is hiding the truth, and I think you know what it is."

"I don't know anything," I gasp as images and memories come flying through my head. I want to make her let go, but I can't. I'm learning far more about her than I care to know, unwillingly stripping her of her secrets. "I came here after they went away. I know nothing about them."

"I don't believe you," Reni says, glaring at me with outright hatred. "You know. You must. You're part of it. If you have nothing to hide, why stay locked away or skulk around like a thief when you come out?"

"Please . . . you're hurting me . . . let me go . . . I don't want to . . ."

"What?" Reni snaps, shaking me. "You don't want to *what*?"

"Learn any more!" I cry.

She frowns. I'm weeping, not because I'm afraid or sad, but because *she* is. I know why she's doing this, why she feels so awful, why she's desperate to uncover the truth.

"You can't change it," I moan. "You can't bring him back. He's dead."

"Who?" Reni hisses. "Grubbs? Bill-E?"

"Loch," I wheeze, and her hands loosen. "You mustn't blame yourself. It had nothing to do with you. He wasn't distracted or angry. That wasn't why he —"

"What are you talking about?" Reni shouts, clutching me hard again.

"You had a fight with him the day he died." She releases me, eyes widening, and the images stop. But I can't let it end there. I have to push on, to try and help her. "You fought about what you were going to watch on television. It was a silly, stupid argument. I'm sure Loch had forgotten it by the time he left. It had nothing to do with his death, I'm certain it didn't."

Reni is trembling. Her lower lip quivers. "How do you know that?" she moans. "I never told anybody *that*."

"It was an accident," I mumble. "It wasn't your fault, so you shouldn't —"

"*How do you know that?*" Reni screams.

I shrug. This hasn't gone like I wanted it to. I had hoped to ease her pain, but instead I've terrified her.

Reni starts to say something, then closes her mouth and

backs off, crying, staring at me as if I'm something hideous and foul. It's how people in my time stared at a priestess or druid if they thought that person was an agent of evil. She backs into a tree, jumps with fright, then turns and flees.

I watch until she vanishes behind the houses of Carcery Vale, then slowly return through the forest for another lonely night with the aloof and morbid Dervish.

SPONGE

✠　　✠　　✠

BERANABUS is only half human. His father was a demon who ravaged his mother against her will. In later life, Beranabus tracked the monster down and slaughtered him. He took the beast's head as a trophy. Held it close to his chest that night and wept for hours, stroking his dead father's face, hating and mourning him in equal measures.

Meera loved Dervish when they were younger. She wanted to marry him and have children. She dreamed of teaching their kids to be Disciples, the entire family battling evil together and saving the world. But she knew he would never father a baby. He was afraid any child of his might catch the curse of the Gradys and turn into a werewolf. So she never confessed her love or told anybody.

Reni saw her mother steal a purse from a store. It was the most shocking thing she experienced until Loch died. She spent many restless nights wondering what else her mother might have stolen, worrying about what would happen if she was caught. She wanted to discuss it with someone, but it wasn't something she could talk about, so she kept it to herself.

I know these things because I've touched those people and absorbed their inner thoughts. I'm a human sponge — I soak up memories.

I became aware of my gift not long after I returned to life. I spent hours with Beranabus that night, hugging and holding him. Memories seeped into me thick and fast, but it was a time of great confusion, and I wasn't able to separate his memories from Bill-E's until later.

It took me a few days to make sense of what had happened. I had all these images of the distant past swirling around inside my head — starting with his wretched birth in the Labyrinth — and I wasn't sure where they'd come from. When I worked it out, I thought it was a temporary side-effect of my miraculous return to life. Or maybe Beranabus had fed his memories to me, to help me cope with the new world.

I didn't touch anybody else until Meera hugged me, in an attempt to comfort me when she found me crying. As soon as we touched, I began absorbing. When I realized what was happening, I broke contact. I felt like a thief, stealing her innermost secrets. The flow of images stopped as soon as I let go.

I learned less about Meera than I had about Beranabus, since we were in contact for only a handful of seconds. The flow of information was fast, but not instantaneous. I took many of her big secrets and recent memories, but little of her younger life.

I hadn't touched anyone since then. I don't like this power. It's intrusive and sneaky, and I can't control it. I don't seem to do any harm. I think the people retain their memories, but I can't be certain. Maybe, if I held on for a long time, I'd drain all their thoughts and they'd end up mindless zombies.

I wish I could experiment and find out more about my unwelcome gift, but I can't without the risk of damaging those I touch. If I was in the Demonata's universe, I could test it on demons — although I'm not entirely sure I want to get inside a demon's head!

Nobody knows about it. I'd tell Beranabus if he was here, but he isn't. I could search for him — I learned what he knew about opening windows when we touched, and I'm sure I could open one myself — but I don't want to disturb him. He's on an important mission and this would distract him. If I'm lucky, the unwelcome gift will fade with time. If not, what of it? I live in seclusion and almost never touch people. I'm sure Reni Gossel won't come back for another face-to-face. What harm can a secluded hermit do to anyone?

✠ I'm in Dervish's study, telling him about Bill-E's problems at school. Bill-E was a shy boy. He found it hard to make friends or fit in. Dervish wants to get to the root of his nephew's difficulties. There's no point — he can't do anything to fix them now — but he's persistent.

"Was it his eye?" Dervish asks. "Billy had a lazy left eye. He often asked me to correct it with magic. If I had, would he have been more confident?"

I shrug.

"Come *on*," Dervish presses angrily. "You know. Don't pretend you don't."

For a moment I feel like telling him to stop pestering me. I want to scream at him to stop obsessing about a dead boy and let me start living a life of my own. It's not fair that I'm forced to spend my days and nights playing these sick games.

But Dervish scares me. He's not big, but he's strong, I can see that in his pale blue eyes. He might hurt me if I crossed him. I'm not sure how far he'd go to keep learning about his nephew. Bill-E loved him unconditionally, so he saw only good things in this balding, bearded man. But Dervish has a tougher side that Bill-E never saw. I'm afraid he might punish me if I annoy him. So I let my anger pass, bow my head in shame, and mutter softly in response to his accusation.

"I don't know, because Bill-E didn't know. It was lots of things, all jumbled up. The death of his mom, his eye, just feeling different. There was no simple reason. If there had been, he could have dealt with it."

Dervish studies me silently, face creased. Finally he nods, accepting my answer. He doesn't apologize for snapping at me — he doesn't see any need to.

"Was he happier when Grubbs came?" Dervish asks, leaning back in his chair. We've talked about this before. We've covered most of Bill-E's life. The only part we've never touched on is the night of his death. Dervish never asks about that.

"Yes," I say, raising my head and flashing a short smile across the table. I know Dervish likes hearing about Bill-E's lighter moments, his friendship with Grubbs, hunting for buried treasure, life with his mom before she died. "Grubbs was his best friend ever, even though they didn't know each other for long."

"Did he suspect they were brothers?"

"No. He sometimes wished they were, but he never had any idea who his true father was. He thought it was you."

Dervish flinches. I knew, even as I was saying it, that I shouldn't. He feels guilty about not telling Bill-E the truth. He doesn't like to imagine he was the cause of any unhappiness in his nephew's short life.

"That's enough for now," Dervish mutters, turning away from me, switching on his computer.

I stand up and edge around the desk. My gaze settles on Dervish's narrow back. I feel an almost irresistible urge to put a hand between his shoulder blades. Partly I want to touch him just to make contact, to say, "I'm real. I have feelings. *See* me." But mostly I want to absorb his memories and secrets, learn what makes him tick. If I knew more about him, maybe I needn't be so afraid. I might find some way to break through the barriers he's erected and make him see me as a person, not just a direct line to his dead nephew.

But that would be wrong. I'd be stealing. I already feel bad for unintentionally taking from Beranabus, Meera, and Reni. I won't do it on purpose, not even to make life easier for myself. So I slide out wordlessly, leaving Dervish hunched over the computer, his secrets intact, the coldness between us preserved.

FRIEND INDEED

✠ ✠ ✠

MEERA Flame roars to a halt in our driveway, turning up out of the blue, the way she normally does. I'm watching television when she arrives. I know it's Meera by the sound of her motorcycle, which is much louder than Dervish's, but I wait for her to knock before going to let her in. I don't want to appear overly desperate for company.

"Hey, girl, looking good," Meera laughs, giving me a quick hug before I can duck. She breaks away quickly, spotting Dervish on the stairs. I don't take much from her, but what I do soak up is new, memories I hadn't absorbed before. It seems like every time I touch a person, I steal something fresh. That's useful to know.

"How have you two been?" Meera shouts, taking the stairs three at a time. She grabs Dervish hard, halfway up the giant staircase that forms the backbone of the house, and hugs him as if he was a teddy bear.

"We've been fine," Dervish replies, smiling warmly. He

never smiles at me that way, but why should he? I'm an interpreter, not a friend.

"Sorry I haven't been by more. Busy, busy. It must be spring in Monsterland — demons are bursting out all over. Or trying to."

"I heard," Dervish says. "Shark has been in touch. It sounds bad."

Meera shrugs. "Demons trying to invade are nothing new."

"But in such numbers . . ."

She shrugs again, but this time jerks her head in my direction. Dervish frowns. Then it clicks — "Not in front of the girl. You might frighten her." I see a small, unconscious sneer flicker across his lips. He doesn't think of me as a girl, certainly not one who can be frightened by anything as mundane as talk of demons. But he respects Meera's wishes.

"Come on up," he says. "We can discuss business in my study."

"To hell with business," Meera laughs, pushing him away. "I'm here to let my hair down. I thought it was time me and Bec had a girls' night in. I bought some lipstick, mascara, a few other bits and pieces I thought might suit you," she says to me. "We can test them out later, discover what matches your eyes and gorgeous red hair. Unless you don't want to?"

"No." I grin. "That would be coolio."

Dervish winces — that was one of Bill-E's favorite words — but I don't care. For the first time in months I have something to look forward to. I experience a feeling I haven't known for ages, and it takes me a while to realize what it is — happiness.

✠ We eat dinner together, which is a rarity. I normally dine alone. Eating is one of the few pleasures I've been able to relish since my return. I love the tastes of the new world. I never imagined anything as delicious as fish and chips, pizza, sweet-and-sour chicken. The strange flavors baffled and repulsed me to begin with, but now I look forward to my meals as I never did before.

After dinner Meera banishes Dervish to his study, and the two of us shut ourselves in my bedroom. Sitting on the edge of my huge four-poster bed, Meera teaches me the basic tricks of applying makeup. It's harder than I imagined, requiring a subtle wrist and deft flicks of the fingers. We try different shades of lipstick, blush, eyeliner, and mascara. It all looks strange and out of place to me, but Meera likes the various effects.

"Didn't people wear makeup in your day?" she asks, working on my eyelashes for the fourth time.

"Nothing like this. The warriors were the most intricately decorated. Many had tattoos, and some used to color their hair with blood and dung."

"Charming," Meera says drily, and we laugh. She runs a hand through my hair and tuts. It's longer and wirier than it's ever been. "We must do something with this. And pierce your ears."

"I'd like that." I smile. "I couldn't grow my hair long or be pierced before."

"Why not?" Meera asks.

"I was a priestess's apprentice," I explain. "Priestesses

couldn't marry, so we weren't meant to make ourselves attractive."

"I bet that was a man's idea!" Meera snorts.

"Actually it was practical. Our magic worked best if we were unsullied."

"You mean you lost your powers if you made out with a guy?" Meera asks skeptically.

"Yes."

"No way," she snorts. "I've made out plenty and it hasn't done me any harm."

"It's true," I insist. "Things were different. Magic was in the air, all around us. It wasn't like when a window opens now. We were more powerful than modern mages, but we had to live a certain way to tap into the magic. Love of any kind was a weakening distraction."

"Hmm," Meera says dubiously, brushing my hair from left to right. I'm soaking up memories each time she touches me, but contact is brief so I'm not taking too much. I try not to absorb anything at all, to block her memories, but I can't.

"You sound like Billy sometimes," Meera says casually. "You said 'coolio' earlier, and 'weakening distraction' was the sort of thing he'd say too."

"There's a lot of him in me," I admit. Bill-E spoke much faster than I did, and he used odd words sometimes. I find myself mimicking him. It isn't intentional.

"I have his handwriting too," I confess, lowering my voice to a whisper. "I never wrote before. I wouldn't have been able to without Bill-E's memories to show me how. When I write, I do it the way he did, exactly the same style."

"I wonder if you have the same fingerprints?" Meera says.

"No." I frown, studying the tips of my fingers, recalling the whorls from before. "This is my flesh. I moulded it into my own shape. On the outside there's nothing of Bill-E left. But in here . . ." I tap the side of my head.

"That must be weird for Dervish," Meera chuckles. I go very quiet. She applies new lipstick in silence, then says, "Dervish never talks about you. I haven't been able to phone often, but whenever I call, I ask how you're doing. He's always vague. Says you're fine, no problems."

I grunt sarcastically.

"I don't know about your time," Meera says slowly, "but in today's world, girls love to share. Boys don't so much — they bottle things up inside, hide their pain even from their best friends. But girls know that a problem shared is a problem halved."

"Bill-E hated that cliché," I tell her. "He thought if that was true, all you had to do was tell your problem to dozens of people. Each time you told it, the problem would be halved, until eventually it would be of no real importance."

"That definitely sounds like Billy," Meera laughs, then looks at me seriously. "If I can help, I will, but first I need to know what's troubling you."

I chew my newly painted lower lip, wondering how much — if anything — I should tell her. She's Dervish's friend, loyal and once in love with him. Maybe she can only see his side of things and will turn against me if I . . .

No. She's not like that. Meera's criticized Dervish before when she thought he was in the wrong. She believes in being honest with everyone. I've no guarantee that she'll side with me, but from what I've absorbed, I believe she'll give me a fair chance.

"He's only interested in Bill-E," I whisper, then fill her in on all that's happened since I stepped out of the cave, only holding back the information about my gift, since that has no bearing on what's been going on with Dervish.

She listens silently, her brows slowly creasing into an angry frown. "The idiot," she growls when I finish. "I guess anyone in his position would want to know what was going on inside Billy's head, but he's taken this way too far. Who does he think he is, treating you like dirt?"

She stands up, fire in her eyes, and strides towards the door. My heart leaps with excitement — she's going to confront Dervish and subject him to a tongue-lashing. Brilliant! But then she slows, stops, thinks a moment, and turns.

"No," she says quietly. "I can't say anything to him about this. *You* have to."

"Me?" I cry, disappointment almost bringing tears to my eyes.

"I can take you away from here," Meera says, returning to my side. "Dervish is no kin to you, so you don't have to stay with him."

"Actually," I correct her, "we are distantly related."

She waves that away. "Like I said, I can take you from him, but I don't think you'd be any happier. If you run away now, you'll always be running. You need to talk to Dervish, make him see you're not Billy's ghost but a real child with real needs. I wouldn't treat a dog the way Dervish has treated you."

"He doesn't do it on purpose," I mutter, surprised to find myself sticking up for him. "He's sad and lonely."

"So are you!" Meera exclaims. "If I was in your place, I'd have set him straight long ago. But you're just a girl. You were afraid to hurt his feelings . . . maybe afraid of what he might do if he lost his temper?"

I nod softly, amazed that she can read me so easily.

"I've known Dervish a long time," Meera says. "He's not as shallow as he must seem. You've caught him at a bad time, the worst of his life. He's lost Billy . . . Grubbs . . . that horrible Swan cow didn't help matters." Dervish had been in love with Lord Loss's assistant, Juni Swan. He'd thought she was a wonderful, kind-hearted woman. When he learned the truth in the cave, he killed her.

"Any other time, Dervish would have welcomed you warmly," Meera continues. "But he's mixed up and you've become part of all that's wrong with his life.

"That has to change," she says sternly. "He can't carry on like a spoiled child. If he can't see sense himself, we have to make him. *You* have to. Because you're the one who lives with him. I could shake him up, but he'd feel guilty and shameful, and that might makes things worse. You need to sort this out yourself." She smiles encouragingly and nods at the door.

"What . . . now?" I stammer.

"No time like the present." She grins.

"I don't know what to say," I protest.

"You'll think of something," she assures me.

"But what if you're wrong? What if he doesn't want to hear from me? What if he only wants access to Bill-E?"

"He can't have it," Meera says softly. "Billy's dead. Dervish has manipulated you to hide from that, but he can't anymore. It's not healthy. Now quit stalling, get up there, and put him in his place. And remember" — she grins — "he's only a man. They're the inferior half of the species. He'll be putty in your hands."

WAKING THE DEAD

✠   ✠   ✠

I trudge up the stairs to the third floor, nervous and hesitant. I don't want to do this. I can't think of anything to say. I wish I'd kept my mouth shut.

Except Meera's right. This *is* unacceptable. I've been silent too long. The old Bec wouldn't have tolerated such disrespectful treatment. I remember when I addressed the men of my village and insisted they let me go with Goll and the others on their mission to find out where Bran came from. Conn — our king — was against it, but I stood firm. If I can stare down a king and tell him what I think, I can certainly face Dervish.

The door to his study is open. I enter, rapping on the heavy wood as I go in. The room is protected from strangers by spells. Dervish never taught me the spells, but I found them easy to break. I don't have the power I experienced when I first came back to life — the cave was filled with energy that I could tap into — but I'm much more advanced than any present-day mage.

Dervish is reading a book about werewolves. Someone in our family bred with demons many generations ago. As a result, lots of our children transform into savage, mindless beasts who must be executed or caged for life. Various family members have searched for a cure over the centuries. Dervish is the latest, but he's had no more luck than the others.

It's possible *I* might turn one day, but I think I'll be able to fight it. Grubbs got the better of his wolfen genes. He's part of the Kah-Gash, and the magic of the weapon gave him the power to reject the change. I suspect I have that same power.

Dervish looks up and squints. "Is that what passes for fashion now?"

I touch my face automatically. "Does it look awful?"

"No." He forces a thin smile. "I was only teasing. You look good." It's the first compliment he's ever paid me. The small act of kindness gives me confidence. I walk around the room, studying the books on the shelves and weapons on the wall. I take down a small sword and swing it experimentally.

"Careful," Dervish says. "That's real."

I whirl the sword over my head and chop down an imaginary opponent. I wasn't supposed to practice with swords, but I did when nobody was watching. Satisfied that I haven't lost my touch, I return the sword to its holder.

"Where's Meera?" Dervish asks.

"Downstairs. She went to get something to eat."

"I'll join her. I'm feeling peckish." He stands up and heads for the door.

"No," I stop him. "We have to talk."

"Later." He scowls, waving me away.

I whip the sword off the wall again, take careful aim, then send it flying across the room. It tears through the leather panel on this side of the door and slams it shut. Dervish leaps away, giving a yelp of astonishment. He looks back at me, shocked.

"We. Have. To. Talk."

"Since you put it so politely . . ." He returns to his chair, eyeing me warily. He glances at the sword buried in the door. Its hilt is still quivering. "Were you sure you wouldn't hit me when you threw that?"

"No," I admit.

"What if you'd struck me?"

I grin tightly. "I'm a healer. I could probably have patched you up."

Dervish strokes his beard, eyes narrow. "What do you want to talk about?"

I stroll to the chair where I usually sit and drag it around to the side of the desk, so I'm closer to Dervish. I hunch forward in the chair, maintaining eye contact. The words come by themselves.

"You never ask about Bill-E's last day or his final thoughts."

Dervish stiffens. "I don't think we need to discuss that."

"Why don't you want to know?" I press.

"Did Meera put you up to this?" he says angrily. "She has no right. It's none of her business."

"No," I agree. "It's *our* business. And it's time we dealt with it."

"What do you mean?"

"You want all of Bill-E, his life from start to finish, wrapped up neatly like a birthday present. I can't give you that unless I tell you about the end, what he felt in the cave, how he reacted to the news that Grubbs was his brother, that you'd lied to him all those years, that you allowed him to be killed."

"I didn't allow anything!" Dervish shouts. "Grubbs did what he had to. There was no other way. If there had been, do you think I would have let him . . . do that . . . to Billy?" He's shaking.

"You're right," I say softly. "It *was* necessary. Bill-E knew that too. He didn't understand everything about the tunnel and the Demonata, but he saw your pain. He knew you still loved him, that you had no choice. He died without bitterness."

Tears well up in Dervish's eyes. His hands are trembling as he nervously tugs at his beard. "He must have hated me," Dervish moans. "I betrayed him. I didn't tell him when his father died. He believed *I* was his dad. I should have —"

"He was disappointed," I interrupt. "He wanted you to be his father because he loved you so much. But that disappointment didn't change his love for you. In fact, in the middle of the madness, when he thought Lord Loss was going to slaughter you both, that love grew stronger than ever. He even found time to joke about it, but he couldn't tell you because he was gagged."

"*Joke?*" Dervish echoes, tears trickling down his cheeks.

"When Lord Loss told him you were only his uncle, Bill-E wanted to say, 'Damn! I guess this means Grubbs gets half of your money now!'"

Dervish laughs and sobs at the same time.

"He was afraid," I continue, recalling Bill-E's memories. "But he didn't resent you or Grubbs. He knew you lied because you didn't want to hurt him. He wished you'd been truthful, but he didn't hold your deception against you."

"What about at the very end?" Dervish croaks. His fingers are balled up into fists. "Did he know what Grubbs planned? Did he guess we were going to . . . *kill him*?" The final two words emerge as a choked whisper.

"Yes," I say sadly. "Bill-E was no fool. He saw it in your eyes."

"Did he hate us?" Dervish cries.

"No. He blamed Lord Loss and bad luck, not you and Grubbs. In fact . . ."

"Go on," Dervish says when I pause.

"He was pleased you were there. He was glad he was with the two people he loved most. He didn't want to die a lonely death. He thought there was nothing worse than being alone."

I'm crying as well now. I want to stop. I don't want to hurt Dervish anymore. But I have to say it. I have to make him see.

"I don't want to be alone either," I weep. "I hate it, Dervish. Loneliness is horrible. I had sixteen hundred years alone in the cave. I thought I'd suffer forever, no escape, no company, not even the release of death to look forward to.

"When I finally walked free, I thought I'd never be alone again. But I have been, and it's awful, maybe even worse than in the cave. At least there I didn't have any hope. But now that I'm so close to people . . . yet alone anyway . . . nobody to talk to or share my feelings with . . ."

"What do you mean?" Dervish says gruffly. "You have me. We talk together every day."

"No," I sniff. "You talk to Bill-E. You look straight through me. I don't think you even know I'm there most of the time — you just hear Bill-E's voice. You only care about a dead boy. You might as well be one of the dead yourself for all the interest you pay to the living . . . to *me*."

I'm crying hard, wiping tears from my face with both hands. Dervish is doing the same, looking at me and really seeing me — *me,* not a shadow of his dead nephew — for the first time.

"I didn't know," he groans. "I just missed Billy so much. I . . . I've been stupid and hurtful." He manages a weak, shivering grin. I smile back shakily. He thinks for a moment. Then, looking as awkward as a boy on a first date, he holds out his arms. I don't want to steal memories from him, but I need to be hugged, more than I ever needed a hug before. So I stretch my own arms out in response, my heart hammering with hope and joy.

Before we can embrace, the door to the study crashes open. A wild-eyed Meera bursts into the room. She slips but grabs the handle and keeps her footing. "We're under attack!" she screams.

Dervish and I stare at her.

"We're surrounded!" she yells.

Dervish's face clouds over. "Demons?" he growls, stepping out of his seat, fingers bunching into fists.

"No," Meera gasps. A howl fills the corridor behind her. *"Werewolves!"*

FIGHT

✠   ✠   ✠

THERE'S a moment of total, frozen disbelief. Then Dervish grabs a sword from the wall and pushes past Meera. I follow close behind. I try to pull the sword I'd thrown earlier out of the door, but it's stuck tight. While Meera hurries to get a weapon of her own, I step into the corridor after Dervish, working on a spell, not sure if it will work — there's so little magic in the air to draw on.

I hear panting. It comes from the far end of the corridor. Something growls and something else yaps angrily in reply. No sight of them yet.

Meera steps out behind us, swinging a mace. She's stuck a knife in her belt. No trace of the gentle woman who was applying makeup only minutes ago. She's all warrior now.

"How many?" Dervish asks without looking back.

"At least three. They entered through the kitchen. I'd been snacking. I was just leaving, so I was able to jam the door and stall them. If they'd burst in when I was at the table . . ." She shakes her head, angry and scared.

The first of the creatures sticks its head around the corner. It's recognizably human, but twisted out of normal shape. It has unnatural yellow eyes. Dark hair sprouts from its face, and its teeth have lengthened into fangs. They look too large for its mouth — it must have great difficulty eating.

It skulks into the corridor, growling. Long, sharp fingernails. More muscular than any human. Hunched over. Covered in stiff hair. Naked. A male. Another two creatures appear behind the first, a male and female. The second male is larger than the first, but follows his lead. His left eye is a gooey, scarred mess. Maybe that's why he's not the dominant one.

As the once-human beasts advance, I step ahead of Dervish and Meera. I try draining magic from the air, but there's virtually nothing to tap into. In my own time, these creatures would have been simple to deal with. Here, it's going to be difficult.

The lead werewolf snaps at the female. With a howl, she leaps. I unleash the spell as she jumps. It's a choking spell. If it doesn't work, I won't know much about it — she'll be on me in a second and I'm defenseless.

The werewolf lands about a yard ahead of me, but instead of pouncing and finishing me off, she rolls aside, whining, the cords of her throat thickening, cutting off her supply of air. Score one for Bec!

The weaker male attacks on all fours. No time for a choking spell. I bark a few quick words and the creature's fingers grab at each other. He roars with surprise and tries ripping them apart. I mutter the spell again, holding them in place. It's more of a trick than a real spell. It will immobilize the werewolf for less than a minute; then he'll break free and I'll have to think of something else.

But there's the dominant male to deal with first. He's more cunning than the others and makes his move while I'm dealing with the one-eyed beast. He barrels across the floor, howling dreadfully.

Before I can react, Dervish and Meera cut ahead of me. Meera lashes out at the werewolf with her mace, swinging the spiked ball expertly, landing a blow to the beast's right shoulder. Dervish jabs at him with the sword, piercing the creature's stomach.

Neither blow is fatal, but the werewolf screams with pain and surprise and falls back a few steps. He roars at the others, summoning them. The female's throat has cleared — she's back on her feet, and although her cheeks are puffed out, she looks ready for business. Morrigan's milk! In the old days that spell would have been the end of her. Curse this modern world of weak magic.

"We can't get past," Dervish says calmly. "Back up. They were human once. If we're lucky, the protective spells of the study will halt them."

"And if they don't?" Meera asks.

"Fight like a demon," he chuckles bleakly.

We shuffle back through the open door of the study. As soon as we're in, I dart to the nearest wall and grab an axe — the swords here are mostly too big for me.

One of the werewolves howls. The female leaps into the study, fangs flashing, ready to tear us to pieces. But as soon as she crosses the threshold she screeches, clasps her hands to the sides of her head, doubles over, and vomits. She looks up hatefully and reaches for Meera, then screams and vomits again. She rolls out. The males roar at her, but she roars back more forcefully than either of them.

"It worked," Dervish notes dully.

The stronger male approaches the doorway. He sniffs at the jamb suspiciously and leans through. His nostrils flare and the pupils of his eyes widen. He leaps back before he gets sick. Dervish strides forward and slams the door shut.

"What are they doing here?" Meera pants. "Where did they come from?"

"No time for questions," Dervish murmurs, stroking his beard with the tip of his sword. "There are probably others with them, demons or mages. They might break the spells and free the way for the werewolves."

The creatures are scratching at the door, their howls muted by the wood.

"The window," Dervish says. "There are handholds down the wall. We can get out that way."

"Handholds?" Meera asks dubiously.

"Call me paranoid," Dervish says, "but I always like to have an escape route." He crosses to the window and jerks hard on the strings of the blinds, yanking them all the way up. As he leans forward to unlatch the window, I get a sudden sense of danger.

"Down!" I scream.

Dervish doesn't pause, which is the only thing that saves him. Because as he throws himself flat in response to my cry, the glass above his head shatters from the gunfire of several rifles.

Meera curses and ducks low. The bullets strike the wall

and shelves, ripping up many of Dervish's rare books, knocking weapons from their holders. A few ricochet into his computer and laptop, which explode in showers of sparks.

I'm lying facedown, shivering. This is my first experience of modern warfare. I find the guns more repulsive than demons. I can accept the evil ways of otherworldly beasts who know nothing except chaos and destruction. But to think that humans created such violent, vicious weapons . . .

"What's going on?" Meera screams as the gunfire stops. "Who's out there?"

"They didn't introduce themselves," Dervish quips. He's sitting with his back to the wall, beneath the shattered glass of the window. He has the look of a man studying a difficult crossword puzzle.

"We're trapped," I snap. Meera and Dervish look at me. Meera's afraid, Dervish curious. "Do we fight the werewolves or the people with guns?"

"The werewolves would appear to be the preferable option," Dervish says. "We can't fight the crew outside — we'd be shot to ribbons in no time. But whoever set this up will have thought of that. I doubt we'll have a clear run if we get past the werewolves — which is a pretty sizeable *if.*" He gets to his knees and grins. "How about we fight neither of them?"

"What are you talking about?" Meera growls.

"A paranoid person has one escape route, easy to spot if your foe has a keen eye. But a *real* paranoid freak always has a second, less obvious way out."

There are two desks in the study — Dervish's main workstation and a second, smaller table for the spillover. He crawls to that, wincing when he cuts his hands and knees on shards of glass. He reaches it and stands, having checked to make sure no snipers can see him. "Help me with this," he grunts.

Meera and I aren't sure what his plan is, but we both shuffle to his side and push as he directs. The desk slides away more smoothly than I would have thought, given the thick carpet that covers the floor. Dervish stoops, grabs a chunk of the carpet, and tugs hard. A square patch rips loose. Beneath lies a trapdoor with a round handle. Dervish takes hold and pulls. A crawlspace beneath the floor is revealed.

"Where does it lead?" Meera asks.

"There are a couple of exits," Dervish explains. "It runs to the rear of the house. There's a window. We can drop to the ground if nobody's outside. If that way's blocked, a panel opens to one of the corridors beneath us, so we can sneak through the house."

"If we survive, remind me to give you a giant, slobbery kiss," Meera says.

"It's a deal." He grins and slides his legs into the hole.

FLIGHT

✠　　✠　　✠

I don't like the crawlspace. The cramped space and lack of light remind me of the cave. I feel my insides tighten. But I bite down hard on my fear and scuttle after Dervish, Meera bringing up the rear. As reluctant as I am to enter, I'll take a dark, tight space over gunfire and werewolves any day.

Dervish reaches the window at the end of the tunnel. It's semicircular, with thick stained glass. He can see out, but it would be hard for anybody outside to see in. He observes in silence. Ten seconds pass. Twenty. Thirty. I can still hear the howls of the werewolves and splintering wood. The door can't hold much longer. They might not be able to enter the protected study, but when they realize we're not there, they'll come hunting for us. What's Dervish waiting for?

Finally he sighs and turns — there's just enough space. I start to ask a question, but he puts a finger to his lips and shakes his head. I nod bitterly. There must be people with guns outside, or more werewolves. Either way, we can't go via the window. We'll have to try sneaking through the house.

We backtrack past the study, then follow the crawlspace round to the right. A short distance later, Dervish removes a panel and slips through the hole in the ceiling beneath us. He helps me down, grabbing my legs and easing me to the floor. Some of his memories flow into me — mostly about Bill-E — but the contact is brief.

We're in a short corridor on the second floor of the house, close to the hall of portraits, which is filled with paintings and photographs of dead family members, most of whom turned into werewolves. Soft growling sounds come from that direction. Dervish listens for a moment, looks around uneasily, then starts towards the hall. Meera and I dutifully follow.

The hall is a mess of shattered frames, ripped paintings, and photos. In the middle of it all squats a werewolf. He's roughly tearing a large portrait to shreds, stuffing bits of canvas into his mouth, chewing and spitting the pieces out. He's urinated over some of the paintings, either marking his territory or showing undue disdain for the Grady clan.

The werewolf doesn't spot us until we're almost upon him. Then Dervish steps on a piece of frame hidden beneath scraps of paper. It snaps and the werewolf's head shoots up. His growl deepens and his lips split into a vicious sneer. Using his powerful legs, he leaps at us, howling as he attacks. He slams into Dervish and drives him to the floor.

No time to use my axe. I yelp and grab the werewolf's jaw, trying to keep his teeth from closing on Dervish's unprotected throat. Jumbled, fragmented memories shoot from the werewolf's fevered brain into mine. What I learn disturbs me, but I don't dwell on it — I have more urgent matters to deal with. The werewolf's teeth are only a couple of inches from Dervish's jugular vein.

I prepare a spell to force shut the werewolf's mouth, but Meera's faster than me. She takes quick aim, then brains the werewolf with her mace. The werewolf's head snaps to the left. His eyelids flicker. Then he slumps over Dervish and it's simple enough to slide him off.

Dervish is furious when he rises. "I should have seen that one coming a mile away," he snarls, wiping blood from his left arm where the werewolf gouged him.

"You're getting old and slow," Meera taunts him. "What now?"

"The cellar," Dervish says.

"We're going to cage ourselves in and get drunk?" she frowns.

"It connects with the secret cellar," Dervish says impatiently. "That's a place of magic. We can seal the doors and keep our assailants out. Unless they —"

He's interrupted by howls from the floor above. The three werewolves have either broken through the door or heard the howl of the one we knocked out. They're coming. We leap over the unconscious animal and flee for the staircase.

✠ Racing down the stairs, the werewolves no more than a handful of seconds behind. If there are more on the ground floor, or snipers with a clear view, we'll be easy targets.

But luck is with us. We hit the ground without encountering any enemies. The howls and screams of the werewolves pollute the air. It sounds like they're poised to drag us down at any moment, but we can't risk looking back to check.

Dervish hits the light switches as he passes, turning them off, to hide us from the snipers. He hurries to the cellar door, barges through, waits for Meera and me to streak past, then slams it shut and locks it. A werewolf batters into it less than two seconds later. This door isn't as sturdy as the one in the study. It won't delay them long.

We spill down the steps to the cellar, automatic lights flickering on as we hit the bottom. This is where Dervish stores his priceless wine collection. Rack after rack of vintage bottles. Behind one of the racks is a hidden exit and a tunnel leading to a second, secret, cellar.

Dervish cuts through the maze of wine racks, angling for the exit, but we're not even halfway when the door above gives and the werewolves roar down the stairs. We won't make it. And even if we get to the rack ahead of them, the panels won't close in time. They'll be able to surge into the tunnel after us. Not much room for fighting in there.

"You go," I pant, laying aside my axe and turning to face the werewolves.

"Are you mad?" Meera shouts.

"Go!" I yell, grabbing two bottles from a rack. "I'll follow."

Meera starts to argue but Dervish grabs her and shoves her ahead of him. He nods at me to wish me luck, then flees.

I face the onrushing werewolves. I have a plan. Sort of. Not a very good one, but if it works, it'll buy us some time. If it doesn't, the werewolves will soon be digging into Bec burgers.

The wine racks form narrow corridors. Wide enough for one person, but two's tight and three's a squeeze. When the werewolves see me alone, they go wild and rush forward, getting entangled with each other in the inadequate space.

When the dominant male bucks off the others, I toss the bottles at him, then turn and run. I make a left at the end of the corridor, leading the werewolves away from Dervish and Meera — and the only way out.

✠ Running through the cellar. I've managed to keep ahead of the werewolves. If they were human, with full control of their senses, it would be a simple matter for them to ensnare me. A pair could simply circle around and wait for me at the end of any of the narrow corridors. The third could chase me towards the others in about half a minute. Game over.

But these beasts work by instinct. They can't think far ahead. When they have the scent of prey, they can only focus on the chase. So they plough along behind me, slipping and sliding in their haste. I grab bottles of wine as I run, lobbing them at the werewolves. They don't do much damage but every bit helps.

I run into a dead end. I'd been expecting it. Part of the plan. I stop a few feet from the wall, turn and wait. The werewolves gibber with delight when they see I'm trapped. They inch forward, clawed fingers flexing, drool dripping from their fangs.

I've been working on the spell since I started running. There's not much more magic here than upstairs, but hopefully the thin traces will be enough. I wait until the lead werewolf is a yard away, then unleash the spell at the bottles of wine in the racks around me. *"Fly!"* I scream.

The bottles shake in their holders. The werewolves pause warily. The cork of one bottle pops out. Wine sprays from the neck, showering the female. She cringes, then laughs hoarsely, sucks wine from the hairs on her arms, and licks her lips.

A few more corks pop. The werewolves are being showered with first-rate wine. They wipe it from their faces, scowling but unharmed, and nudge forward again. I start to think my plan has failed, then . . .

Dozens of bottles shoot off the racks and slam into the werewolves. The monsters howl with pain and fall to the floor in protective huddles. Glass shatters over and around them, pounding their shoulders, backs and heads. Cuts open and bones break. One bottle smashes most of the fangs in the lesser male's mouth.

I make my move, not waiting for the shower of glass to cease. I scurry up the wine rack to my left, using it as a makeshift ladder. I crouch on top, set my hands against the ceiling and strain with my feet, trying to topple the rack. If it was full of bottles, I couldn't budge it. But it's mostly empty and it rocks nicely beneath me. I sway it backwards and forwards a couple of times, then send it toppling over the werewolves, further confusing, enraging and delaying them.

I leap to the neighboring rack as the first goes over, then hop to the next and the next, like a frog. There's not much space between the tops of the racks and the ceiling. An adult couldn't maneuver up here, but there's just enough room for a wee bec of a girl like me.

The screams of the werewolves are almost deafening in the confines of the cellar. But to my ears, as I hop ever farther away from them, it's like music. The bottles and rack won't stall the werewolves for long, but I don't need much time.

Seconds later I come to the exit. It's normally hidden

behind what looks like an ordinary wine rack. Dervish has opened it and the two halves of the rack gape wide. I can see the secret corridor and Meera lurking within it. Leaping off the rack, I make a neat landing and snap to my feet like a gymnast finishing a complicated routine.

"Cute," Dervish grunts, then smiles and waves me through. I push past and he hurries after me. The mechanical rack slides shut behind us, cutting out the cries of the werewolves and sheltering us from the bloodthirsty beasts. We share a grin of relief, then hurry down the corridor to the safety of the second cellar.

A minute later we arrive at a large, dark door. It has a gold ring handle. Dervish tugs it open and we slip through. It's dark inside.

"Give me a moment," Dervish says, moving ahead of us, leaving the door open for illumination. "There are candles and I have matches. This will be the brightest room in the universe in a matter of —"

The door slams shut. A werewolf howls. Meera and I are knocked apart by something hard and hairy. Dervish cries out in alarm. There's the sound of a table being knocked over. Scuffling noises. The werewolf's teeth snap. Meera is yelling Dervish's name. I hear her scrabbling around, searching for the mace, which she must have dropped when we were knocked apart.

I'm calm. There's magic in the air here. Old-time magic. Not exactly like it was when I first walked the earth, but similar. I fill with power. The fingers on my left hand flex, then those on my right. Standing, I draw in more energy and ask for — no, *demand* — light.

A ball of bright flame bursts into life overhead. The werewolf screeches and covers its face with a hairy arm. Its eyes are more sensitive than ours — perfect for seeing in the dark. But that strength is now its weakness.

As Dervish huffs and puffs, trying to wriggle out from beneath the werewolf, I wave a contemptuous hand at the beast. It flies clear of Dervish and crashes into the wall. The werewolf whines and tries to rise. I start to unleash a word of magic designed to rip it into a hundred pieces. Then I recall what I learned in the hall of portraits. Instead of killing it, I send the beast to sleep, drawing the shades of slumber across its eyes as simply as I'd draw curtains across a window. As it falls, I flick a wrist at it and the werewolf slides sideways and out through an open door, the one it must have entered through before we arrived.

Dervish sits up and looks at the door. "We have to shut it," he groans, staggering to his feet. "Block it off before . . ."

At a gesture from me, the door closes smoothly. Blue fire runs around the rim, sealing it shut. I do the same with the rim of the door we came through. "All set," I grunt. "Balor himself couldn't get through those now."

Dervish and Meera gawp at me and I smile self-consciously. "Well, I *was* a priestess."

Dervish starts to chuckle. Meera giggles. Within seconds we're laughing like clowns. I've seen this many times before. Near-death experiences often leave a person crying or laughing hysterically.

"I wish I could have seen you go to work on those werewolves," Meera crows. "We could hear it, but we couldn't see."

"It's just a pity you couldn't do it some other way," Dervish sighs. "Some of my finest bottles were stored back there."

"You can't be serious!" Meera shouts.

"A Disciple can always be replaced," Dervish mutters, "but a few of those bottles were the last of their vintage."

My smile starts to fade, but then Dervish winks at me. "Only kidding. You were great." He wipes sweat and blood from his forehead, then coughs. "I'm beat. Meera was right — I'm getting old and slow. I need to sit down. I feel . . ."

Dervish's face blanches. His lips go tight and his eyes bulge. He staggers back a step, gasps for air, then collapses. Meera screams his name and rushes to his side.

"What is it?" I cry, whirling around, testing the air for traces of a spell being cast against us.

"Dervish?" Meera asks, holding his arms steady as he thrashes weakly on the floor.

"Who's doing this?" I bellow. "I can't sense anybody. I don't know what sort of a spell they're using."

"Quiet," Meera says. She tugs her cardigan off and slides it under Dervish's head. His face has turned as grey as his beard. His eyelids are closed. His chest is rising and falling roughly.

"But the spell! I must —"

"There isn't any spell," Meera says softly, stroking the tufts of hair at the sides of Dervish's head. She's studying him with warm sadness, like a mother nursing a seriously ill baby.

"Then what is it?" I stumble towards her, stopping short of Dervish's twitching feet. "What's wrong with him?"

Meera looks up. There's fear in her eyes, but it isn't fear of demons, werewolves, or magic. "He's had a heart attack," she says.

WAITING FOR THE CAVALRY

✠　　✠　　✠

HEART attacks were rare in my time. People didn't smoke (tobacco wouldn't be introduced to our part of the world for nearly another thousand years) or eat unhealthy food. Most of us didn't live long enough to suffer the modern curse of middle age. A few of my clan died of weak hearts, but they were exceptions.

Nevertheless, I'm a healer. Once Meera has explained Dervish's condition to me and we've laid him in a comfortable position, I set to work. Without touching him, I feed magic to his heart, softly warming it, keeping the valves open. Some color seeps into his face and he breathes more easily, but he doesn't regain consciousness.

"Will he live?" Meera asks quietly.

"I don't know." I study his face for signs of improvement but find none.

The werewolves are hammering at the door behind us. People are attacking the other door with axes. I direct magic into the wood and walls to keep out the intruders. I also mute the sounds, so we can focus on Dervish and monitor his breathing.

"Can you look after him by yourself for a while?" Meera asks.

"Yes."

She moves away, digs out her cell phone and presses buttons. "Hell! I don't have a signal."

I consider the problem, then mutter a short spell. "Try now."

Meera smiles her thanks, then makes several calls. She doesn't bother with the police. This is a job for beings of magic — the Disciples.

Meera's on the phone for half an hour. I keep a close watch on Dervish. He looks terrible, much older than he did an hour ago. I'll be surprised if he makes it through the next few days.

Meera finally puts her phone away and returns to my side. "How is he?"

"Alive. For now."

"Can you use magic to keep him healthy?"

"I can help. There's more power here than in the house, but it's still limited. If he has another attack . . ." I shake my head.

"Do your best," Meera says, giving my arm a squeeze. "Disciples are on their way. They'll be here within twenty-four hours. We can transfer him to a hospital then."

"In his state, that will be a long time," I tell her. "You should prepare for the worst."

She chuckles weakly. "I'm a Disciple, Bec. We always expect the worst."

We settle back and watch in silence as Dervish quietly duels with death.

✚ After a few hours the sounds of the werewolves and their companions fade. Have they left or are they lurking nearby, trying to tempt us out? No way of telling. Best not to venture forth and chance it. Safer to sit tight and wait for help.

We have to deal with a few practicalities. There's no water or food. We can go without food for a day, but we need water for Dervish. I try finding a spring in the ground below us. There isn't one, but I sense a pipe running overhead, carrying water to the house. Extending my magic, I pierce a hole in the pipe and draw a jet of water through the ceiling. We fill vases and a few of the larger, ornately designed candlestick holders. Then I plug the hole with dirt and a shield of small pebbles. It should hold for a few days. It's a plumber's problem after that.

We can't improvise a drip, so I use magic to ease water down Dervish's throat. Meera feeds it to him from a vase and I make sure he doesn't choke or swallow the wrong way.

"I always hate it when a young person has a heart attack," Meera says. I don't think of Dervish as young, but I guess in this world he isn't old. "It seems so unfair, especially if they're in good shape and have taken care of themselves. Dervish never had the healthiest diet, but he exercised regularly. This shouldn't have happened."

She looks almost as drawn and tired as Dervish. This is hurting her. She still loves him. I know from her memories that nobody ever touched her heart the way Dervish did, even if he was unaware of it.

"Who did you call?" I ask, to distract her.

"Shark and Sharmila," she says. "I tried a few others but they were the only pair who could come."

"Will two be enough?"

"They're two of the best. Do you know them?"

"Sort of. Bill-E met them in a dream once."

She stares at me oddly, so I explain about the movie set of Slawter and a dream Bill-E, Grubbs, and Dervish shared when they thought they were on a mission with Shark and Sharmila. It's a complicated story. Meera knows bits of it, but not all the details. I fill her in, glad to have something to discuss, not wanting to think about Dervish and what he's going through.

A thought grows while I'm talking, and when I finish explaining about Slawter, I make a suggestion to Meera. "I can open a window to the Demonata's universe. We can take Dervish through and find Beranabus. I'll be stronger there. I can do more to help. Beranabus could help too."

"From what I know of Beranabus, he's not the helping kind," Meera mutters, considering the plan. "Could you find him immediately? Take us straight to him?"

"No. We'd have to go through a couple of realms, maybe more."

She shakes her head. "We should stay. Dervish can't fight and we don't know what we'd find. There could be demons waiting for us there."

"I doubt it."

"There might be," she insists. "We don't know who was behind this attack. Maybe it was Lord Loss."

"I don't think so. I touched one of the werewolves. I . . .

I have a gift. I can learn things about people when I touch them."

"What sort of things?" Meera frowns.

"I read their minds. Access their secrets. Absorb their memories. I've been able to do it since I came back to life."

"Have you read *my* mind?" she asks sharply, and I nod shamefully. "How much did you learn?"

"A lot. But I'd never reveal what I know. I wouldn't even have taken it, except I've no choice. Every time I touch someone, I steal from them. I can't stop it."

"Why didn't you tell me?" Meera asks, looking more confused than angry.

"I would have eventually, but there was so much else to deal with. . . ." I shrug it off. "Anyway, I touched one of the werewolves and saw into its mind. It was a jumble, shards of memory all mixed up. I couldn't make sense of most of what I saw. But I learned his name, who he was before he changed, and who he was passed on to."

"Well, come on," Meera says when I hesitate.

"His name was Caspar," I tell her. "He was a Grady. He turned into a werewolf when he was fourteen. His parents did what many of their kin do and turned him over to the family executioners — the Lambs." I know about the Lambs from the memories of Bill-E and Beranabus.

"But the Lambs didn't execute him," Meera says, her expression fierce.

"No. I'm assuming the other werewolves were family members scheduled for execution too. But all of them wound up here."

"The guys with the guns . . ."

"They were probably working for the Lambs."

We stare at each other, then at Dervish lying unconscious by our feet. And the temperature of the room seems to drop ten degrees.

✠ Meera doesn't understand why the Lambs would do this. They sometimes keep werewolves alive, to experiment on them in an attempt to unlock their genetic codes and discover a cure. But only with the parents' permission.

"I can picture them keeping the beasts alive on the quiet," she says. "Very few parents care to commit their children to a lifetime of laboratory misery, even if they've turned into werewolves. It's no surprise if the Lambs told them their kids had been executed, then kept them alive to study.

"But why bring them here to attack us? And how did they organize them? They were working as a team, as if they'd been trained. I didn't think you could do that with werewolves. Even if you could, why send them against *us*?"

That's the key question. According to Meera, Dervish never had much love for the Lambs. They originally formed to execute children who'd turned, but over the decades they acquired more power and branched out into more experimental areas. Dervish didn't approve of that, especially since he didn't think science could find a cure for a magically determined disease.

"The Lambs never liked Dervish either," Meera says. "They thought if he explained more about demons, it might help them with their studies. But they'd no reason to attack him. At least none that I'm aware of."

"Maybe it's me," I mumble. "Grubbs turned into a

werewolf — temporarily — and because of his magical powers, the Lambs couldn't stop him. Maybe they're afraid I'll turn too and become a menace."

"But they don't know you're one of the family," Meera says. "Dervish told them nothing about you. There's something we're missing. . . ."

We spend hours debating the mystery. We get no closer to the truth, but at least it helps to pass the time. During the discussions, I think of another reason why the Lambs might have targeted me. But I say nothing of it to Meera, deciding to wait until the other Disciples arrive, so I don't have to repeat myself.

✠ Someone knocks on the door leading to the yard. Meera and I were both half-dozing. We jolt awake at the sound and I strengthen the magical fields around the doors and walls. Then a man shouts, "Little pigs, little pigs, let us come in!"

"Idiot," Meera grunts, but she's smiling. "It's Shark."

"I know. I remember his voice from Bill-E's dream."

I remove the spells and the battered door swings open. A tall, burly man in an army uniform enters, followed by an elderly Indian woman who walks with a limp.

"Sorry we're late," Shark says, hugging Meera and lifting her off the floor.

"How is he?" Sharmila asks, hobbling directly to Dervish.

"He's been like that since the attack," I tell her. "No change."

She stares at me suspiciously. "You must be Bec. I have heard about you."

"The dead girl who came back to life," Shark says. He's

looking at me oddly. "I thought you'd be more like a boy, considering . . ."

". . . I stole Bill-E's body?"

"Yeah."

"There's nothing of Bill-E left," I tell them. "Except his memories. That's how I know you and Sharmila."

Shark frowns. "I never met him."

"I did," Sharmila says, "but many years ago, when he was very young."

"I know. But he met both of you." I grin weakly at their confusion.

"Bec can tell you about that later," Meera snaps. "What's happening outside?"

"Nothing," Shark says. "All quiet. Your birds have flown the coop."

"You're positive? It isn't a trap, to lure us out of hiding?" Shark shakes his head. "Then let's get Dervish straight to a hospital. We can talk about the attack on the way. But I'll tell you this much — they weren't birds. They were *Lambs*."

✦ Shark and Meera carry Dervish up the steps out of the cellar as gently as they can. Shark grumbles about what he's going to do to the Lambs when he catches up with them. He drove here in a van. There's a hospital trolley in the rear. We strap Dervish down and Sharmila produces a drip and heart monitor. She hooks Dervish up. I watch with interest — it's the first time I've seen such apparatus.

When Dervish is as secure as we can make him, I ask Shark if he's absolutely certain we're not going to be attacked.

"Nothing in life's an absolute," he replies, squinting at the trees, the mansion, the sky. "But if this was a trap, the time to attack would have been when we were moving Dervish up from the cellar. That's when we were most vulnerable. I'm confident we've nothing to fear for the time being."

"Then I've a favor to ask." I feel strange being so forward, but this is no time to be shy. "I can open a window to the Demonata's universe from the cellar. I'd like you to go through and find Beranabus."

Shark blinks slowly. Sharmila is frowning.

"Have you ever been to that universe?" Sharmila asks.

"No."

"Then you do not know what you are asking. It is a place of chaos and peril. We have never been there without Beranabus to guide us."

"I know how dangerous it is," I mutter, flashing on some of Beranabus's many memories of the hellish universe. "But I'll try to open the window to one of the less savage zones. Did Beranabus teach you a spell to find him once you're there?"

"No," Shark grunts. "But Dervish did."

"We have never tested it," Sharmila notes. "What if the window closes and we cannot find him? We will be stranded."

"Dervish might be dying," Meera hisses.

"I have sympathy for Dervish," Sharmila says coolly. "That is why I came when you summoned me. But can Beranabus heal him? And even if he can, why should we risk our lives for his?"

"It's not about helping Dervish," I say quickly before an

argument develops. "We don't know who the Lambs were after. Their target might have been Dervish or Meera, but it was probably *me*."

"What if it was?" Shark asks.

"I'm important," I mutter, feeling embarrassed. "I can't explain — there isn't time — but I'm part of a powerful force that might mean the difference between winning and losing the war with the Demonata."

Sharmila's eyes narrow. "The Kah-Gash?"

"You know about it?" I sigh with relief.

"We helped Beranabus search for a piece once," Shark says. "It wasn't our most successful mission."

"I am not convinced of that," Sharmila says. "I always suspected . . . *Kernel?*" She raises an eyebrow.

My smile broadens. "Yes. He was a piece. Grubbs is another. So am I."

"What are you talking about?" Shark frowns.

Sharmila waves his question away. "Does Beranabus know?"

"Yes."

"Then why are you not with him?"

"He didn't want to keep us together until he found out more about how the weapon works. He thought I'd be safe here. Nobody else knew. At least we didn't think so. But if the attack was directed at me, maybe my secret's out. If that's the case . . ."

". . . Beranabus must be informed." Sharmila nods. "I understand now."

"Care to explain it to the rest of us?" Shark asks, bemused.

"Later." She thinks about it for a few seconds. "I would go but I am old and slow, even when pumped full of magic. Besides, I know a lot about healing, so I might be of more help here. Meera?"

"I'm not as strong as you," Meera says.

"But you are younger and faster. In this instance that is important."

"I don't like that other universe," Meera mutters.

"Neither do I. Believe me, I would not send you there lightly."

"You really think this is necessary?"

Sharmila nods slowly. Meera sighs and agrees reluctantly.

"Shark?" Sharmila asks.

"You want me to place my life on the line without knowing the reason why?" he scowls.

"Yes."

His scowl disappears and he shrugs. "Fair enough."

"You understand how time works in that other universe?" Sharmila asks me. "It can pass quicker or slower than it does here. They might find him in a matter of minutes as we experience time or it could be several months."

"I know. But we don't have a choice. I'd go myself, except if it's a trap . . ."

". . . demons might be lying in ambush for you. Very well. Let us not waste any more time. I will stay with Dervish. Shark and Meera will accompany you to the cellar." She smiles tightly at Shark. "You have been to hell in a bucket before, my old friend. Now it is time to go there without the bucket."

✠ In the cellar. I'm working on a spell to create a window to the demon universe. It's an area Beranabus goes to frequently — his father took his mother there when he abducted her. Because Beranabus has opened a window to that realm many times, it's a relatively quick and easy procedure, though it still takes me an hour.

As I complete it, a thin lilac window forms in the cellar. I get a shiver down my spine. I never saw a window like this in my own time, but Beranabus has been through thousands of them. He acts like it's no big thing, but he loathes these demonic passageways. He always expects to die when he steps through, having no real way of knowing what's lurking on the other side.

"Will you be all right staying here with Sharmila?" Meera asks.

"Yes."

"We should come with you and enter the demon universe later," Shark says. "If the Lambs attack you on the way to hospital . . ."

"I might not be able to open a window there," I explain. "It's easier if I'm in an area of magic."

"Even if Beranabus doesn't come with us, we'll return," Meera says.

"He'll come." I smile confidently.

"Because you're part of the Kah-Gash?"

"Yes. But also because we're old friends."

"I didn't think Beranabus had any friends," Shark grunts.

"Maybe not now. But he was a boy called Bran once and I was his friend then. He'd do anything for me."

"You're sure of that?" Meera asks.

I think about the night I sat with Beranabus and absorbed his memories. He always wears a flower in a buttonhole, in memory of me. "I'm certain."

"Right," Shark says, rubbing his hands together. "Keep a light burning — we'll be back in time for supper."

Shark steps through the window. Meera smiles wryly, then moves to hug me. I take a step backwards.

"I'd rather not touch. I don't want to steal any more memories from you."

"Don't be silly," Meera says, wrapping her arms around me. "If things go badly over there, you can remember my life for me."

We grin shakily at each other, then Meera slips through the window after Shark. I wait a couple of minutes in case they run into trouble and need to make a quick retreat. Then, as the window breaks apart, I douse the lights and climb the steps to help Sharmila escort Dervish to the hospital.

PART TWO

✠   ✠   ✠

WARD DUTY

SNAPSHOTS OF BERANABUS II

✤ ✤ ✤

AFTER the death of the Minotaur, the years of wandering began. Beranabus had no difficulty finding his way out of the Labyrinth. He had explored every last alley of the maze. It had been home to him and he knew it intimately.

Sunlight disturbed the boy. Having grown up in darkness, the world of light seemed unbearably bright. He tried to brave the glare, but the pain was too great. Weeping, he retreated. Not knowing about the outside world, he assumed it would always be this bright, the way the Labyrinth had always been dark.

When the sun dropped and the sky darkened, Beranabus cautiously crept out again. It was still a lot lighter than he liked, but he was able to adjust to the shades of the night world. He looked back once at the Labyrinth, feeling sad and alone, remembering the good times, riding high on the Minotaur's shoulders, feeding on the fresh blood and meat of the beast's kills. Then, reluctantly, he turned his back on his childhood home and set off to explore this new, peculiar world.

✠ Beranabus was a simple child. He couldn't speak. He could understand some of what other people said, but not everything. Most of the world was a mystery to him, filled with beings who made a huge amount of noise and fought lots of battles for no reason that he could see.

He shouldn't have lasted long in such a hostile environment. But Beranabus had a remarkable gift, which saved him when he first entered the world — he could tame the wildest of creatures and find friendship in the most unlikely places. Wherever he went, he was accepted. People took him in to their homes, gave him passage on carriages and boats, fed and clothed him, treated him with kindness and love.

Many took pity on the boy and sought to keep him and raise him as their own. But Beranabus liked to wander. After the confines of the Labyrinth, the open space of the world intrigued him and he wanted to see more of it. So, without any real design or purpose, he always moved on, slipping away from those who yearned to root him, feeling nothing more for them than he did for the dirt beneath his feet or the air whispering through his hair.

✠ One day, when the boy was on the brink of his teenage years (although he'd been alive for more than two centuries), he witnessed a demon on the rampage. The monster had crossed near a small village and was busy killing as many humans as it could before it had to return through the window of light to its own universe.

The demon reminded Beranabus of the Minotaur. He had come a long way from Crete and seen much of the world and *its people, but this was the first demon he'd encountered. The savage beast amused him. It was shaped like an octopus, but with several heads of various animals and birds. He liked the sounds the humans made when the demon killed them, and the patterns their blood created as it arced through the air in streaks and spurts.*

He watched the massacre for a few minutes, as if enjoying a show. The demon saw him but didn't attack, mesmerized by the boy's strange aura, as all other dangerous creatures had been.

Murder meant nothing to Beranabus. He didn't understand concepts of right and wrong, good and evil. His mind was a muddled grey zone. Many had tried to teach him, but all had failed. The only difference in his head between a living person and a corpse was that the former was more entertaining.

When the demon retreated, Beranabus was curious to see what the beast would do next, whom it would kill, what sort of mischief it would get up to. So he stepped through the window after the demon, out of his mother's universe, into the much darker and spectacularly violent playpen of the Demonata.

✦ *Beranabus had a whale of a time in the universe of his father. The demons were far more bloodthirsty than humans. They could kill each other in ways men had never dreamed of. Death didn't have to be swift either. A demon master could torment a lesser demon for decades . . . hundreds of years . . . millennia if it wished.*

Beranabus drifted with delight from one crazy realm to another. He didn't need to sleep much or eat and drink. And he aged at an even slower rate there than on Earth. He was part of a universe of marvels, and it seemed he could go on enjoying it for as long as he liked.

He had to be careful, of course. He could tame most demons, but some resisted his charms and tried to capture him. Beranabus was uneducated, but he wasn't stupid. He knew what pain and suffering were, and while he loved to observe the torment of others, he had no wish to become one of the tortured.

That was when he discovered his gift of speed. He could run faster than any demon that chased him. So, on the occasions where he could not tame a demonic beast, he fled, laughing gleefully as he ran, safe in the knowledge that the demon would soon lose interest in him and abandon the chase for easier pickings. In the Demonata's universe there was always something else to kill.

✠ *Windows were plentiful. Although demons could only cross to the human world with the aid of a malevolent magician or mage, many could travel from one zone to another in their own foul realm. Their universe was an endless parade of blood-drenched worlds and galaxies. Some of the stronger demons could even create infinite self-contained zones of their own, which somehow nestled within the larger unified demon universe.*

Whenever Beranabus tired of a realm, he searched for a window and usually found one quickly. He never worried about what he would encounter on the other side. Uncertainty and potential peril all were part of the delight of his life.

Eventually, inevitably, he stepped through a window to

the human world. He knew he'd crossed universes as soon as he sniffed the air — it was less charged with magic. Instinct urged him to retreat, but curiosity tempted him on. A long time had passed — he could tell from the buildings around him — and he wanted to see what the people were like, how they varied from those he'd known, whether they died any differently.

In the demon universe, windows could remain open indefinitely. He assumed that was the case here as well, but he was wrong. He spent only a handful of minutes in the town — just enough to realize that demons were far more interesting than humans — but when he returned to the spot where the window had stood, it was gone. He was stranded, a captive of the world where he had first begun.

✠ When Beranabus discovered to his dismay that windows of magic were incredibly rare on this world, he traveled with fiery intent, hitching lifts with armies and traders, riding and sailing to the farthest reaches of civilization. He was desperate to return to the universe of the fantastical demons.

This was the first time Beranabus's brain stirred actively. Until then he had wandered neutrally, observing whatever he chanced across. But now he went in search of something specific and moved with a purpose, carefully choosing those he traveled with, deliberately setting out to explore fresh locations full of promise.

As his brain took its first developmental staggers forward, he unconsciously learned a few words and mimicked the speech of those he hitched rides with, although most of the time he only uttered gibberish. His mind was still a confused, *chaotic country, full of storms and whirlpools. But he had taken the first steps towards understanding and intent, and the world — the universes — would never be the same for him again.*

✠ *Some years later the boy found himself on an island, set at the westernmost limit of the known world. Demons had broken through and established a permanent tunnel. Thousands of monsters had flooded the land. They were terrorizing the locals, laying siege to the villages and towns, slaughtering all in their path.*

Beranabus eagerly trudged around the country in search of the tunnel, admiring the torments perpetuated by the Demonata. But as he moved from one village to another, a dim sense of unease grew within him. He felt nothing substantial for the dead humans he saw every day, nor the terrified living who would soon be butchered by the demons. But something about their plight troubled him. He had changed inside, and although the change was slight, it had altered his view of slaughter.

Human suffering was different from what he'd seen in the demon universe. On this world, those who survived mourned for the dead. Demons laughed at death, but people here cared about their families and friends. Beranabus found it hard to wring pleasure from their pain. It was too . . . human.

His unease made him more determined than ever to find the tunnel and leave this world. In the Demonata's universe he could revert to his old ways and simply revel in the merciless mayhem. He didn't like the way he was changing. The world was more fun if you could enjoy it with complete abandonment, untouched by the misery of others.

As he instinctively learned and practiced new words, Beranabus sometimes tried to mutter his name aloud. He could remember what his mother called him, but he couldn't pronounce it. The closest he could get was "Bran." Those who heard him took it to be his name. Having a name was a new experience, and Beranabus found it oddly comforting. He started to mutter "Bran" every time he met someone new, so they would know what to call him, but his mind was still a jumbled mess and he occasionally forgot.

After a time, as he was resting in a village on a tiny island at the center of a lake, Bran came in contact with a druid called Drust. Bran sensed that Drust was also on a mission to find the tunnel. So, instead of moving on, he remained in the village and even let Drust send him to find others to assist him on his quest. Bran didn't know that the druid planned to close the tunnel, and he wouldn't have cared if he did. As long as he could race through before it shut, back to the universe of the demons, he would be content.

Finding people to help Drust wasn't easy. The druid was very precise in his request, demanding not just warriors but a being of magic. Ideally he needed a fellow druid or priestess, but failing that, he'd settle for someone who had a healthy magical talent, even if it was undeveloped.

Bran didn't understand all that, but Drust meddled with the boy's mind, magically implanting his requirements. Bran had the power to counter the druid's influence, to break the spell Drust had woven around him. But he needed Drust to find the tunnel, so he accepted the druid's orders.

He tried in his befuddled way to recruit a band for Drust in several villages without success. At most there were no people of sufficient magic, and at two where there were, the people dismissed him as a mad child.

Finally, late one evening, he came to a ringed fort. He could sense a person of magic within — a young woman — but had no great hope of attracting her to his cause. Squatting outside the village wall, he waited for the curious warriors to come and examine him, as they had everywhere else. But when the door opened, the magician accompanied the warriors, and for Bran everything altered.

The woman — little more than a girl — looked no prettier than any other her age. Her power was unremarkable. The land was littered with hundreds like her. In his time Bran had sniffed with disinterest at beautiful princesses and powerful priestesses.

But something about this girl struck him hard. He showed no outward sign of it, and couldn't even express his feelings clearly to himself. But the moment he saw the girl — Bec — he fell madly and completely in love. It was love he had not known since his early years with the Minotaur, love he would never know again until she returned to him after many centuries of captivity. And although he couldn't voice his feelings, he knew on some deep level that he would do anything for this girl, kill if needed, give his own life for hers if he must.

So it was that Beranabus at last, without intention or knowledge of what it would mean, put his demonic interests behind him and became a real human.

A MAN'S GOTTA DO

✢　✢　✢

DERVISH is hooked up to all manner of machines. He's wealthy, so he gets his own room and the best possible care and attention. The machines are incredible, so intricately designed, capable of detecting tiny flaws that Banba and I never could have, no matter how strong our magic. When the doctors and nurses aren't busy, I ask about the various consoles and monitors, memorizing their answers. If I was ever granted the freedom to pursue a normal career, I'd work day and night to master these machines and become a modern-day healer.

It's been four days since Dervish's heart attack, three since we brought him to the hospital. The doctor who first examined him was furious that we'd waited so long to admit him. But she was soon replaced by a surgeon who knew of the Disciples, and Sharmila was able to explain the reasons for our delay.

Dervish's room is on the fifth floor, two floors down from the top of the hospital. It's close to an elevator shaft. There are armed guards stationed outside, but they keep their weapons hidden discreetly. Sharmila arranged for them to be here. The Disciples have many useful contacts.

Most of the guards are cold and distant, focused on their watch. But a couple chat with me during the quieter moments, and one — Kealan — is outright friendly. Kealan's one of two trained medics who alternate shifts. They're more closely involved with us than the other guards — if we have to move Dervish in an emergency, Kealan or the other medic will handle any medical complications.

Sharmila or I have been with Dervish the whole time, except when his doctors are examining him. A cot has been set up in a corner of the room, and we take turns sleeping there.

Dervish has flickered into consciousness a couple of times, but never for long, and he hasn't said anything or showed signs of recognition. His doctors aren't sure what state his brain is in. They don't think he suffered serious mental damage, but they can't say for certain until he recovers. *If* he recovers.

Sharmila has discussed the situation with her fellow Disciples. She considered going straight after the Lambs, but we're still not absolutely certain they were behind the attack. And even if they are directly involved, we don't know whom they're working with or what we might walk into if we go after them. Better to wait for Beranabus.

I don't mind waiting. This is the calm before the storm. I'm sure the peace won't last. We'll soon have all the action we could wish for, and more. I'm enjoying the lull. In my previous life I was eager to leave the confines of my village and explore the world. If I could do it all again, having seen the terrors of the wide blue yonder, I'd probably stay at home and keep my head down. Not the most heroic of responses, but I never wanted to be a hero. I'd much rather lead an ordinary life. Normal people don't know how lucky — how blessed — they are.

✠ Sharmila is talking to Dervish, chatting away as if he's listening to her every word. You're supposed to do that with people who are comatose. Doctors say it can help, and even if it doesn't, it can't do any harm.

I've tried speaking to Dervish, but what can I say? I don't want to tell him about Bill-E — that period of our relationship is over — but we don't have much else in common. I've shared some of my previous life, described the rath where I lived, my people, our customs. But I don't know how interested Dervish is in ancient history. I worry, if he can hear, that I'm boring him.

Sharmila's reminding Dervish of their adventures in the demon universe when they were younger. She recalls their encounter with Lord Loss, Kernel surprising them all with his knack for opening windows, the loss of Nadia Moore — who would later resurface as the treacherous Juni Swan. I've heard most of it before and I'm feeling restless.

"Do you mind if I stretch my legs?" I interrupt.

"Not at all," Sharmila says. "I will call if I need you." She gave me a walkie-talkie a couple of days ago, so we could keep in touch. Cell phones aren't allowed inside the hospital.

Kealan is on duty with three other guards outside the

room. They don't ever seem to get bored, even though they just stand and stare down the hall all the time. Kealan asks how Dervish is, then if I want to play a game of cards.

"Maybe later" — I smile — "if you're still here."

"Where else would I be?" he chuckles wryly. Kealan's the only guard who looks unsuited to his job. I'm not sure why he got into this military business. I think he'd be much happier just being a medic. Maybe the army trained him and he has to serve a number of years with them before moving on.

I stroll through the various levels and wards of the hospital. I know the building well by this stage, and many of the doctors and nurses have got to know me. They give me treats and make small talk when they're not busy. It's been quiet here since I came, and some of the staff consider me a good luck omen. I'm even allowed into areas that would normally be off-limits, like the maternity ward on the second floor. It's my favorite part of the hospital. I love watching cute, wrinkled babies, gazing into their innocent eyes, most the color of a clear, blue sky.

But I head in a different direction on this foray, winding my way up to the roof. I've been stuck inside all day. I need fresh air. I'm also hoping to see a helicopter. It's exciting when one lands. I'd love to go up in one, but I suspect even good luck omens don't get to hitch rides in hospital helicopters.

It's evening. An overcast, patchy sky. I spend a long time watching the sun vanish and reappear from behind drifting clouds. My old teacher, Banba, thought you could read signs of the future in the movements of clouds, but I've never been able to predict anything from them. Still, when I've nothing else to do, I like to try.

"Where are you, Beranabus?" I whisper, hoping the clouds will answer. "How long will it take you to come?"

I'm not sure what we'll do if he doesn't find us soon. We can't wait forever. Where will we go when Dervish recovers or dies? Back to Carcery Vale? To stay at Sharmila's home or with other members of the Disciples? Into the universe of the Demonata to search for Beranabus?

I feel guilty when I think about Shark and Meera, and the mission I sent them on. It was necessary to summon Beranabus. If the attack happened because I'm part of the Kah-Gash, he needs to know. But how likely is that? Maybe I secretly sent them to get him because I was missing my old friend.

A breeze blows in from behind me, tickling the hairs on the back of my neck. I shiver with delight and snuggle into the wind as if it was a giant cushion. Then I pause. This is a warm breeze, not like the cold blasts that whipped across the roof the other times I've been up here. And it's coming from a different direction. It feels unnatural.

I focus, senses locking on the currents of air, mentally tracing the breeze back to its origins. I wasn't good at this in the past, but my talent has blossomed since I died. My mind bounds off the roof like a magical hound and hurtles towards the ground. As it draws level with the first floor, it veers through a broken window, one that's been shattered from the inside out.

It comes to a halt in the center of the room and my eyes

snap open. There's a mage, a man of weak magic, but strong, evil intent. And in front of him stands a panel of light — a window into the universe of the Demonata. As I probe it with mental tendrils, I sense figures hurtling through. As much as I wish otherwise, it's not Beranabus or his Disciples. I'm a long way removed, but even from up here I'm able to tell that the creatures setting foot on our world aren't human. They're demons!

✠ I'm on the walkie-talkie before I take my first step. "Sharmila! Answer! It's an emergency! Over."

She replies as I'm taking my third step. "What is happening? Over."

"Demons. On the first floor. Move Dervish."

"Damn!"

Racing down the stairs, I feel the air fill with magic, flooding up through the building from the open window. That's good for me — more power to tap into — but it's also good for the Demonata. I try keeping track of the window, to get an idea of how many demons we'll have to deal with, but it's hard when I'm running. I'd stop and concentrate, but there's no time for that.

"Hey!" a nurse shouts as I hit the fifth floor and race towards the elevator shaft, where I spot Sharmila, the four guards, and Dervish. "No running!"

I don't stop. I reach Sharmila a few seconds later. The elevator has arrived. The guards are rolling Dervish in on a hospital gurney. I'm relieved Kealan was able to unhook Dervish from his banks of machines so quickly.

"Where are they?" Sharmila asks.

"I'm not sure. They entered on the first floor, but I don't know —"

"How many?"

"Give me a moment." I step into the elevator after the guards and Dervish. I focus as the doors close . . . my senses seep down through the building, searching for demonic targets. . . .

With a gasp I jam a hand between the doors just before they close. The panels slide apart automatically.

"What are you doing?" Sharmila snaps.

"They're in the shaft," I hiss. "Three of them. Climbing the cables."

"Out!" Sharmila barks at the guards. As they roll Dervish back into the corridor, the nurse who shouted at me hits the scene.

"Where are you going with that patient? You can't move him without a doctor's orders. I'm calling the —"

Sharmila waves a hand at her. The nurse's eyes flicker, then she turns and walks away.

"The stairs?" Sharmila asks.

"More of them there. Eight or nine."

Her face pales. "Can we fight them?"

"If we have to. They're not strong. But there are so many of them. . . ."

Balazs — the smallest of the guards — is on his walkie-talkie, talking softly but quickly. He finishes and clips it to his belt. "The roof," he says calmly. "A helicopter will be with us in five minutes."

"Bec?" Sharmila asks. "The elevator or stairs?"

I concentrate. The demons in the shaft are making fast

progress. Those on the stairs are moving slower, pausing to pick off a few unfortunate nurses who get in their way.

"The stairs," I decide, hurrying ahead of the guards to open the door.

Gabor and Bence — the other two guards — push the gurney to the foot of the stairs, then each takes an end. They raise the wheels off the floor and start up the steps. Kealan moves alongside them, monitoring Dervish.

"You two go ahead," Balazs says to Sharmila and me, taking out a pair of pistols. "I'll hold off the demons."

"You cannot kill them with bullets," Sharmila says.

"I know," Balazs says softly. "But I can slow them down."

Sharmila starts to object, then nods curtly and flees up the stairs, no longer limping, using magic to move freely and swiftly.

"Do you want me to stay and help?" I ask Balazs.

"No," he says. "You'll serve more good if you stay with Dervish."

"You'll die," I note sadly.

"Dying's my job." He grins bleakly. "Now get the hell out of here and let me do what I'm trained for."

I stand on my toes and give him a quick hug. I get flashes of his mother's face. She was mauled by a demon. It took her several hours to die. A slow, painful death. Balazs is determined not to suffer as she did.

Releasing the doomed guard, I chase after the others, feeling the demons close on us from beneath.

✠ We've just passed the seventh floor, heading for the exit to the roof, when the gunfire starts. We pause, even the guards who are used to situations like this. Then we press on. By the time we crash through the doors at the top of the stairs, the hail of bullets has stopped.

Bence and Gabor check their watches. Their frantic eyes reveal how desperate the situation is. Unholstering their weapons, they silently head down the stairs.

"Where is the helicopter coming from?" Sharmila asks as Kealan wheels Dervish towards the landing pad.

"Nearby," Kealan says. "We'd have kept it here, but there wasn't space. The hospital helicopters took priority."

"Nobody said anything to me about that," Sharmila huffs.

"We make our own plans," Kealan says. "We don't discuss them with civilians, not even Disciples. No offense meant."

"None taken."

Guns blare on the staircase.

"How much longer?" I shout.

Kealan checks his watch. "A minute. Maybe two."

I dart back towards the stairs. "Bec!" Sharmila screams.

"Don't worry," I pant. "I'm not going to fight them."

I didn't absorb any of Beranabus's magic when we touched, but I learned a lot of his spells. There are many I can't use — there's more to magic than knowing the right words — but some I can. Reaching the doors at the top of the stairs, I draw upon the ancient magician's years of experience and prepare a holding spell.

Bullets are still being fired on the stairs. "Gabor! Bence!" I yell. "Come back!"

There's no response. A few seconds later the guns stop. There's the sound of scurrying footsteps — but not human feet. Grimacing, I unleash the spell and block the doorway with a shield of magical energy.

The first demon appears. It has a square, bloodstained head. Dozens of eyes. Three mouths. A tiny body. It leaps at me, wild with bloodlust, but crashes back off the shield. It snaps at the web of energy, trying to tear it apart with its teeth, but the barrier holds.

I back away from the doors, focusing my power. This is the first time I've tried this spell and the effort involved is greater than I thought. By tapping into the magic in the air, I can hold the shield in place, but I won't be able to maintain it for long, especially not with demons snapping and clawing at it. But I don't need much time, just a minute. It should be enough.

I'm halfway to the landing pad when I hear the whirring sound of helicopter blades and spot the craft humming towards us. I feel a sense of triumph like a hard ball in my gut. In their own universe, some demons are able to fly. But flight is difficult here. Strong demons might manage short bursts, but the beasts who crossed aren't especially powerful. Once we're in the air, we'll be safe.

I don't let thoughts of escape make me careless. I stay focused on the shield. I'm tiring fast — there's so little magic in this world. I can hold it for another couple of minutes maybe, but that should be all the time we —

Something powerful slips through the window on the first floor. Not a demon, but not human either. A beast far more dangerous than any of the others. It snaps questions at the mage who's been holding the window open, then howls at the top of its voice. The cry echoes up the stairs and corridors. The demons struggling with the shield pause to screech in response.

The new, mysterious monster throws itself through the shattered glass window of the room, digs its claws into the wall, and scurries upwards, scaling the building like a jet-propelled spider. I start to yell a warning to Sharmila, but before the words have left my lips the creature hauls itself over the edge of the roof and leers at us maliciously.

The beast has the shape of a woman, but her skin is a mass of blisters and sores. Pus oozes from dozens of cracks and holes in her jellyish flesh. Her mouth is a ragged red slit, her eyes two green thimbles in a putrid, yellow mockery of a face. A few scraps of hair jut out of her head. She wears no clothes — the touch of any material would be agony on flesh so pustulant and tender.

The creature points at the helicopter, which has almost completed its descent, and barks a phrase of magic. The blades stutter, then stop. The helicopter shakes wildly, spins around a few times, then plummets several feet shy of the building. It makes a sharp, screaming sound as it drops. Then it hits the ground and there's an explosion, louder and more brutal than any movie bang ever prepared me for. Glass explodes in all the nearby windows. A giant ball of flame belches up into the sky, turning the evening red. Meera and Kealan are thrown to the floor and the unconscious Dervish slides off his gurney.

Only the woman and I remain standing, using magic to shelter ourselves from the force of the explosion. I sense the shield give way behind me and demons spill onto the roof. But I don't care about them now. I have a more dangerous foe to contend with.

The most frightening, bewildering thing is, I *know* her. It's impossible — I saw her die — but I'm sure I'm right. Her voice when she cast the spell was familiar and, misshapen as she is, if I squint hard, I can make out the lines of her original face. I saw and heard her in the cave the night I returned to life. Even if I hadn't, I'd know her from Beranabus's memories. She was his assistant once — Nadia Moore. But now she serves a different master, our old foe Lord Loss. And she calls herself . . .

"Juni Swan," the semi-human monster gurgles, bowing with cynical politeness. Her lips move into a jagged line as she straightens — I think it's meant to be a smile. "Delighted to kill you."

She flicks a hand at me and the ground at my feet bellows upwards in a pillar of molten, burning tar.

UP ON THE ROOF

✠ ✠ ✠

INSTEAD of trying to fight the black, scorching geyser, I ride
it upwards, using the force of the blast to propel myself high
off the roof and clear of the sizzling liquid. My lower legs are
spattered and the tar burns through my flesh, but those are
minor wounds. I can heal them easily once I've dealt with
the more pressing dangers.

I land in a crouch, using magic to soften the blow. I don't
take my eyes off the mutated Juni Swan. She's watching me
with a wicked, twisted smirk. Her eyes blaze with a mad hatred. I don't know how she cheated death — it shouldn't be
possible — but she hasn't come back cleanly. She's been reduced to a staggering, seeping carcass of cancerous cells.
Her body looks like it's been eating away at itself for the past
six months. The pain of holding it together and clinging to
her frail grasp on life must be unendurable. I'm not surprised she's lost her grip on sanity.

"Little Bec," she sneers, her words coming thick and
syrupy through the wasted vocal cords of her throat. "My

master killed you once, but you returned to life, like me. I wonder if you'll come back again?"

"Who is she?" Sharmila screams, back on her feet, helping Kealan up.

"Juni Swan!" I shout.

"Juni . . . ? You mean *Nadia*?" Sharmila gasps, staring with horror at this mockery of a human form.

"Not anymore." Juni gives a sick chuckle, taking a few tottering steps towards us. Fleshy smears from her feet stick to the rooftop. She winces every time she moves. Her body is fragile, but her power is great. She's stronger than she was in the cave.

Kealan fires three times at Juni. The bullets stop in midair, inches from her scarred, glutinous face. "Pretty little butterflies," she murmurs, turning two of the bullets into silvery swollen insects — but these butterflies have oversized mouths and sharp teeth. She flicks a finger at them and they fly back to their source. I try to deflect them, but I'm too slow. They latch on to Kealan's eyes and dig in. He screams and collapses, blind within seconds. The butterflies continue chewing through to his brain.

I want to help Kealan, but I dare not turn my gaze away from Juni, even for an instant. She makes the third bullet rotate a few times, then sends it shooting at the middle of Sharmila's forehead. The old Indian lady redirects it with a short flick of her wrist and the bullet buries itself in the roof.

The demons from the staircase have split to surround Sharmila and me. There are six around me, five around Sharmila. The twelfth — the square-headed demon —bounds over to Kealan and finishes off the unfortunate guard.

"You should have stayed dead," Juni says, closing on me. The demons are keen to attack, but they're holding back, wary of Juni Swan. They must be under orders not to strike before she does.

"How's my broken-hearted boyfriend?" Juni asks, turning her head to study Dervish. She gasps with pain, a chunk of her neck ripping loose. Grimacing, she pushes the fleshy fillet back into place and uses magic to seal it. Part of me feels sorry for her. This is a terrible way for anyone to exist.

"Leave Dervish alone," Sharmila growls.

"Or what?" Juni jeers.

Sharmila tenses her legs, then leaps over the demons around her. She lands between Juni and Dervish, grabs the gurney, jerks off a side bar, and hurls it at Juni, jagged end first. The tip strikes Juni's gooey face and drives through the rotting flesh and bone. She shrieks, her head snapping back.

Sharmila rips another bar loose to use against the demons who are scurrying after her. She thinks she killed Juni, but she's wrong. As Sharmila turns, Juni yanks out the bar. Bits of yellowy-pink flesh trickle from the hole it leaves behind.

"You'll have to do better than that," Juni giggles, launching the bar at Sharmila. It hits her right shoulder, lifts her off her feet, and sends her sailing across the roof. She smashes into one of the staircase doors. The bar thrusts through her flesh and deep into the wood, pinning her to the door. She screams in agony, blood pouring from her shoulder and mouth. She tries to wriggle free, but can't, pinned in place like a captured moth.

I'm truly scared now. It took a lot of power to throw a steel bar that hard. I don't have anywhere near that kind of strength, not in this world. In a one-on-one battle with Juni Swan, I won't stand a chance.

Juni fixes her insane, bloodshot eyes on me again. There's a tiny insect in the corner of one socket, chewing at the rotting flesh of her lower eyelid. "It's a pity," she mutters. "I hoped Grubbs would be here. I wanted to kill him at the same time as Dervish."

"He'll be here soon," I lie, trying to keep the tremble out of my voice. "Kernel too. And Beranabus." Her expression twitches when I mention the name of her old master. "You'd better get out of here before —"

"Billy Spleen was a bad liar," she cuts me off, "but you're worse. I wonder if you'll squeal like he did when I kill you."

"Bill-E didn't squeal. I know. I was there."

"So you were. I forgot."

A crab-shaped demon with a cat's face jabbers something and shuffles towards me.

"Not yet," Juni snarls. "I want to torture her first."

The crab snaps at her and Juni scowls. "I don't care what he said. I . . ." A look of disgust crosses her face. "No. You're right. We'll kill them and get out of here. But not before we've had some sport." She waves at Sharmila. "The Disciple is yours, along with the humans below. Leave the girl and Dervish to me."

The demons peel away. Three of them — the fastest — converge on Sharmila and set to work on her legs, gobbling the flesh of her feet and shins, pausing only to dance diabolically to the rhythm of her tormented screams. The square-headed demon is still feasting on the remains of Kealan. The rest barrel down the stairs, back into the bowels of the hospital.

Juni smiles horribly. "Alone at last," she wheezes.

I say nothing, backing away slowly, trying to think of a way out of this. Down the wall and through the window on the first floor? But Lord Loss is probably waiting on the other side. I'm surprised he didn't cross with Juni. Maybe he wasn't sure whom he'd find and didn't like the prospect of a run-in with Beranabus.

"I won't kill you immediately," Juni says, edging after me, leaving a trail of slimelike, bubbling flesh, blood, and pus behind. "I'll keep you alive awhile, like Sharmila." She points at the wailing woman. The monsters have stripped the flesh from her bones beneath the knees and are slowly moving up her thighs. Sharmila should have fainted by now. They must be keeping her conscious with magic.

"I'll kill you," I sob.

"I think not," she chuckles. "You're the one who'll perish tonight. But I'll kill Dervish first. I'll wake him and make sure he knows what's happening. Can't let him sleep through his death. I'll bring him round, no matter what shape his brain is in. Slaughter him nice and gruesomely. Then finish you off."

The square-headed demon finishes with Kealan and heads down the stairs to find more pickings below. I set my gaze on it, bark a quick spell, and send it flying at Juni's head. She deflects it upwards. It squeals as it shoots into the air.

"You'll have to do better than that, little —"

I yank my walkie-talkie out and toss it at the demon. When it hits, I make it explode. The demon explodes too and its blood rains down on Juni. Before it splatters, I transform it into acid. It hits with a burning hiss. Juni shrieks and tries to brush away the acidic blood. A drop splashes over her left eye and it sizzles like an egg frying in a pan, washing the insect loose. She howls with rage, hate, and pain.

I race towards the staircase. I'll grab Sharmila if I can and flee. A window between universes can't last more than a few minutes, even with a mage working to keep it open. If I can evade capture for that long, Juni and the demons will have to return to their own —

The door next to Sharmila tears free of its hinges and smashes into me, knocking me down. I saw it coming at the last second and erected a partial shield, otherwise I'd be dead. But it cracks a few ribs and bones and almost punctures my lungs.

As I struggle to my feet, the door rises into the air, hovers a moment, then explodes in a hail of splinters. Again I manage to construct a weak barrier around me, which stops most of the splinters from penetrating. But dozens hit home and pierce me, a few just missing my eyes, a long, thick shard almost staking me through the heart like a vampire.

"Look at the pitiful hedgehog," Juni gurgles as I writhe on the roof, trying to make the splinters pop out of my flesh. She's cleansed herself of the acidic blood, looking no worse than she did before. "All pink, bloody, and spiky. I'm going to slice your stomach open and keep you alive while I fish your guts out. How do you like the thought of feeding on your own intestines before —"

A ball of crackling energy strikes Juni hard. She shrieks with shock as she's blown through the air, coming to a stunned stop a few feet from the edge of the roof. As she staggers to her feet, she looks for her assailant. I look too and find him standing near the gurney, leaning on it for support, exhausted and the color of death, but fired up for action — *Dervish!*

"Leave my girl alone, you crazy bitch," he growls, unleashing another bolt of energy. This one hits Juni in her distorted chest, blasts her off the top of the building, and she yowls like a cat on fire as she drops.

KIDS' STUFF

✠   ✠   ✠

DERVISH takes out two of the demons feasting on Sharmila, using magic to pop their brains like grapes. They're dead before they hit the floor. The third glances up, sees that Dervish has beaten off Juni, and disappears down the stairs.

Dervish limps across the roof. I'm closer and faster, so I get to Sharmila before he does. She's slumped unconscious. I leave her that way and pour magic into her legs to stop the worst of the pain and cauterize the open wounds. The demons have stripped her to scraps below her thighs. Most of the bones are intact, but I can't restore the flesh around them.

"Will she live?" Dervish barks, hobbling close to inspect the damage.

"Maybe. But I can't do much with the legs. She'll lose them."

He sighs, eyes drifting, then snaps back into focus. "Where are we? What's happening? Be quick."

"You had a heart attack. We're on the roof of a hospital.

You've been in a coma for four days. Demons are attacking. Juni Swan was leading them."

"I thought I killed her in the cave," he growls.

"You did. She came back."

"How?"

"I don't know." I gulp. "You didn't finish her off this time either. I can sense her. She's wounded but alive."

"Is she returning for more?" he asks eagerly, fingers twitching, for a moment looking half as crazy as Juni did.

"No," I answer, tracking her mentally as she slips through the window on the first floor. "You must have hurt her. She's gone back to the demon universe."

"Damn." He stares around, eyes going vague. He looks like he's about to collapse. I step forward to support him but he comes alert again and waves me away. "We're exposed. We have to get out of here."

"There are at least nine demons downstairs," I tell him. "We could create a barrier, block their route to the roof . . ."

"What if more cross and climb the walls?" he grunts. "No, we have to move." He takes hold of the bar pinning Sharmila to the door. "Can you make sure she doesn't feel this?"

"I'll do my best." Once I'm focused, I nod and he pulls sharply. The bar rips out of the wood and Sharmila's flesh. She moans softly, but I use magic to numb the pain, and she falls silent again. Dervish slides around and takes Sharmila on his back, holding her arms crossed around his neck.

"Will you be able to carry her?" I ask. He's sweating and trembling.

"Only one way to find out," he mutters, and staggers down the first of the stairs, back into the demon-infested building.

✠ We make our way down through the levels of the hospital. The air throbs with the screams and moans of people who were struck by glass shards when the windows shattered. We spot some of them as we descend. They're milling around helplessly while nurses and doctors try to calm and help them.

I spy a demon on the fifth floor, chasing a man with a cast on his right leg. I look at Dervish, silently asking if we should help. He shakes his head. "We can't do anything," he wheezes. "I'm running out of strength. We need to save our energy — we might have to use it to break free."

"We weren't sure you were going to recover," I tell him as we stumble down the next set of steps.

"Maybe I wouldn't have. But they made the mistake of opening a window too close to me. The magic flooding through hit me like a wave and revived me."

"Magic brought you back to life?"

He nods. "And it's keeping me going. Which is fine. But when the window closes, I'm toast. That's why we have to get out of here. The demons will have to return to their own universe or perish when the window shuts, but there might be soldiers or werewolves waiting to move in."

We trudge on in silence, Dervish panting, struggling to support Sharmila. His legs are shaking badly. Even with all the magic in the air, he can't last very long. He might drop before we make the ground. If he does, I'll have to leave him. Sharmila too. I'm not a coward, but it would be foolish to stay. In desperate times you have to act clinically. Dervish and Sharmila understand that and would only curse me if I let myself be slain for no good reason.

As we come to the second floor I spot a lizardlike demon slithering through the door from the stairs. I motion for Dervish to stop, and we wait until the creature has passed. As we come abreast of the door, I glance through the circular window. There are two more demons with the lizard. One looks like an anteater, only it's bulkier and has several long snouts. The other is some sort of demonic insect with a heavy golden shell, the size of a large dog.

As I watch, they kill an elderly woman and a nurse, then claw open a door and slip into a ward out of sight. Dervish has moved on, but I remain where I am, a wretched feeling in my gut.

"Hurry," Dervish huffs. "We're nearly there."

"Dervish . . . ." I say hesitantly.

"What?" he snaps.

"There are three demons."

"So?"

"They've gone into the maternity ward."

Dervish shuts his eyes and sighs. He looks more like a corpse than one of the living. I think he'd be happier if he was dead. I wait for him to say something, but he only stands silent and unresponsive.

"The babies," I whisper. "We can't let them slaughter babies."

"We should," Dervish croaks. "It's the first law of being a Disciple — if you don't stand a decent chance in a fight, *run*."

"I'm not a Disciple."

"I am." He pulls a weary face. "But to hell with it." He gently lays Sharmila down, stretches, and groans, then steps up past me, pushes the door open, and holds it like a doorman. "Ladies first."

✠ The ward rings with the sound of crying, but it's the natural noise of babies who have been abruptly awoken. I'm sure the mothers are terrified, but they're trying to control their fear so as not to alarm the little ones.

The half-dissolved bodies of two nurses line the hallway ahead of us. Fresh corpses. They must have tried to stop the demons. I pray we have more success.

Dervish is looking a bit better than he did on the upper floors. We're close to the window — the mage has managed to keep it open, curse him — so there's more magic in the air. He moves ahead of me, his legs no longer shaking quite so badly. His gown gapes at the back. I can see his bottom. That would make me smile any other time, but nothing strikes my funny bone at the moment.

We find the insect demon terrorizing a young mother in a room on our left. She's no more than three or four years older than me. Another woman's with her. The pair are shielding the baby from the beast. It's snapping at them, relishing their fear, stretching out the terror.

"Hey, roach!" Dervish calls. The demon turns and Dervish fires an energy bolt at it. The demon shoots across the room and smashes into the wall. But it recovers quickly and propels itself at Dervish. He catches it and they roll to the floor, wrestling. "Go!" he shouts at me.

My instinct is to help him, but the other demons could

slaughter several babies while we battle with this one. Better to advance. Even if I can't kill them, I can delay them and hope the window closes while we're fighting.

I let the women escape with the baby, then hurry down the hallway. I catch evidence of an attack in a room to my right — a small hand lying on the floor near the door, attached to nothing — but I don't stop to probe. Best not to look too closely at something like that.

The anteater demon staggers into the corridor ahead of me unexpectedly, erect on two legs, holding a squealing baby over its head. I see the child's mother frantically reaching for it through the doorway, but she's being held back by the other demon. She's too shocked to scream.

As one of the anteater's snouts attaches itself to the baby's face, I use magic to rip the infant away. It flies safely into my arms. A boy. I absorb his memories of birth as I set him down, then turn to face the demon.

The anteater's snarling. It barks a command and the lizard joins it. The mother rushes out of the room, darts past all three of us, snatches her baby, and flees. I remain focused on the demons, waiting for them to make the first move.

The anteater rears back two of its snouts and spits twin tendrils of mucus at me. I deflect the missiles and they spatter the walls on either side, burning into them. One thing about demons — they love to spit acid.

The lizard scurries towards me, using its tail as a whip to accelerate. When it's a yard away, it gives an extra hard *thwack* with its tail and shoots up at me, jaws stretched wide to clamp around my throat.

I made my fingers hard while the lizard was advancing,

transforming them into a makeshift blade, a trick I learned from Beranabus. Now I duck and swipe at the lizard's stomach. But it realizes my intention and sucks in. I open a shallow cut, but it's only a flesh wound.

The anteater is on me before I can react. It wraps two snouts around my chest, one around my neck, and lashes at my face with the others. The one around my neck is the worst. It digs in tight, cutting off my oxygen.

I drop to my knees, then spring into the air like a frog. I hammer hard into the ceiling, knocking chunks out of it and shaking up the anteater. Its snouts loosen, and when we hit the floor again I jerk free and leap to my feet.

I create a small ball of fire and blow it up one of the anteater's snouts. When it hits the demon's head, an eye bursts. The anteater squeals and stumbles away. Before I can pursue it and finish it off, the lizard bites down on my hip and jabs its forked tongue deep into my flesh.

I shake the lizard off, but I feel poison in the wound. Deadly, fast-acting. If I don't deal with it immediately, I'll be dead within seconds.

I use magic to counteract the poison, expelling most of it from my system and sapping the sting from the rest. I'm successful, but the healing spell is draining. There's not much fight left in me. The demons sense my weakness and move apart — the anteater's recovered from his nasal mishap — then advance, trapping me against a wall. I summon what's left of my power, but before I can unleash a spell against them . . .

A window of orange light opens a few yards away. The demons gape at it. I prepare for the worst, expecting Lord

Loss or Juni to emerge. This is the end. I'm going to die here, surrounded by demons and newborn babies. My only hope is that some of the young survive. If they do, I won't have entirely wasted my life.

A man steps through the window, and my heart leaps.

"Bran!" I shout.

A grave-faced Beranabus winks at me, then glares at the quivering demons. "I bet you thought you'd make off with easy pickings," he growls. "You meant to harvest this crop of babies and gorge yourselves, aye?"

An anxious Grubbs steps through the window, followed by Kernel, who looks different somehow, and a cautious Shark and Meera.

"What do the pickings look like now?" Beranabus asks.

The demons turn and flee. Kernel, Shark, and Meera set off after them.

"Dervish?" Grubbs snaps.

"Back there," I pant. "Hurry. He was fighting a demon. I don't know —"

Grubbs is gone before I finish.

Beranabus squats beside me. "Hello, little one," he says softly. Then he hugs me and I weep into his shoulder. I absorb more of his memories as I clutch him, but I don't care about the theft. I'm just delighted that, despite all the odds, it looks like I'm going to end this evening of butchery alive.

THE SPLIT

✠   ✠   ✠

Back on the roof. The Disciples killed several demons and the mage who'd been helping them. A few of the beasts fled through the window before it closed. The rest died here, helpless without magic, choking to death on our clean human air, then rotting like the disgusting, hellish globs that they are.

The patients and staff inside the hospital are safe, although not many remain. They're being evacuated. A huge operation, still under way. I watched it with Beranabus while we were waiting for the others to join us. I'm impressed by how swiftly the people of this time can move in an emergency, how selflessly they rise to the occasion and risk all to help.

Sharmila is lying close by, unconscious. Beranabus removed her thighbones and has been working on the tattered flesh, sealing off veins and arteries, mending nerve endings where he can, destroying others to lessen the pain that Sharmila will experience when she wakes.

Dervish is sitting nearby on the gurney, head bowed, feebly stroking his beard, shivering from shock and the cold night air. His heart has held, but Beranabus had to help him climb the stairs, carrying him as Dervish had earlier carried Sharmila. Meera is sitting beside her dear friend, watching over him like a faithful hound.

Shark's by the staircase, ready to turn away anybody who ventures up this far. He enjoyed tackling the Demonata and ripping a few to pieces. He's delighted with his evening's work.

I'm bringing Beranabus, Grubbs, and Kernel up-to-date, telling them about the werewolf attack, my gift of soaking up memories, what I sensed from the werewolf I touched, the assault at the hospital. Shark and Meera hadn't told them much — there wasn't time. It took them several weeks in the demon universe to find Beranabus. Thankfully they passed through zones where time moves faster than it does here.

"You're sure the Lambs masterminded the attack in Carcery Vale?" Grubbs asks. He's grown an inch or two since I last saw him and towers above everybody. But he's lost some weight and doesn't look so healthy. His red hair has grown back — he was bald in the cave — but has been scorched bare in a few patches. There are dark bags under his eyes and an ugly yellowish sheen to his skin. He looks exhausted and distraught.

"I can't be certain," I admit. "We didn't see any humans. Sharmila wanted to go after the Lambs once Dervish was safe, but we decided to wait until we'd discussed it with you. The werewolves *might* have been the work of some other group. . . ."

"But they were definitely teenagers who'd been given to the Lambs?" Grubbs presses.

"Yes. At least the one I touched was. I don't know about the others."

"They must have been," he mutters. "I've never heard of anyone outside our family being inflicted with the wolfen curse. But why?" He glances at Dervish. "Have you been rubbing Prae Athim the wrong way?"

"I haven't seen her since she paid us that visit before *Slawter*," Dervish answers. "I've got to say, I don't have much time for Prae, but this isn't her style. I could understand it if they were after something — you, for instance, to dissect you and try to find a cure for lycanthropy — but there was nothing in this for them. Those who set the werewolves loose wanted us dead. The Lambs don't go in for mindless, wholesale slaughter."

"But if not the Lambs, who?" Kernel asks. The bald, chocolate-skinned teenager was blind when I last saw him, his sockets picked clean by demonic maggots. He's restored his eyes in the Demonata universe, but his new globes don't look natural. They're the same blue color as before, but brighter, sharper, with tiny flickering shadows moving constantly across the surface.

"I think Lord Loss was behind the attacks," I answer Kernel's question. "Maybe he realized I was part of the Kah-Gash and wanted to eliminate the threat I pose, or perhaps he just wanted to kill Dervish and me for revenge. The attack tonight by Juni Swan makes me surer than ever that he sent the werewolves. It can't be coincidence."

"Juni Swan," Beranabus mutters guiltily. "I'd never have

thought poor Nadia could turn into such a hideous creature. I don't know how she survived. Your spirit flourished after death, but you're part of the Kah-Gash. Juni isn't. Lord Loss must have separated her soul from her body some way, just before her death. That's why he took her corpse when he fled. But I don't understand how he did it."

He broods in silence, then curses. "It doesn't matter. We can worry about her later. You're right — Lord Loss sent the werewolves. I cast spells on Carcery Vale to prevent crossings, except for in the secret cellar, where any demon who did cross would be confined. Even if he found a way around those spells, he would have been afraid to risk a direct confrontation. If he opened a window, the air would have been saturated with magic. You and Dervish could have tapped into that. You were powerful in the cave, stronger than Lord Loss in some ways. He probably thought humans and werewolves stood a better chance of killing you. But that doesn't explain why the Lambs agreed to help him. Or, if they weren't Lambs, how they got their hands on the werewolves."

"Maybe he struck a deal with them," Dervish says. "Promised them the cure for lycanthropy if they helped him murder Bec and me."

"Would they agree to such a deal?" Beranabus asks.

"Possibly."

"Prae Athim's daughter turned into a werewolf," Grubbs says softly. "She's still alive. A person will go to all manner of crazy lengths when family's involved." He winks at Dervish.

"An intriguing mystery," Beranabus snorts. "But we can't waste any more time on it. We have more important matters to deal with, not least the good health of Dervish and Miss

Mukherji — they'll both be dead soon if we don't take them to the demon universe. Open a window, Kernel."

Kernel starts moving his hands, manipulating patches of light that only he can see. That's his great gift — he can open a window in minutes instead of hours or days, to any section of the demon universe. In the past he couldn't work his magic on this world, but he seems to have developed since I last saw him.

"I'm not going," Dervish says.

"You can't stay here," Beranabus retorts.

"I have to. They attacked me . . . my home . . . my friends. I can't let that pass. I have to pursue them. Find out why. Extract revenge."

"Later."

"No," Dervish insists. "Now." He gets off the gurney and weaves to his feet. Meera steadies him. He smiles at her, then glares at Beranabus.

"It would help if we knew," Meera says in support of her friend. "The attack on Dervish and Bec might have been a trial run. The werewolves could be set loose on other Disciples."

"That's not my problem," Beranabus sniffs.

"There's been a huge increase in crossings," Meera says. "We've seen five or six times the usual activity in recent months. The Disciples are stretched thinly, struggling to cope. If several were picked off by werewolves and assassins, thousands of innocents would die."

"It might be related," Kernel says, pausing.

"Related to what?" I ask, but Beranabus waves my question away. He's frowning.

"This could be part of the Shadow's plan," Kernel presses. "It could be trying to create dozens of windows so that its army of demons can break through at once. We'll need the Disciples if that's the case — we can't be everywhere at the same time to stop them all."

"Maybe," Beranabus says grudgingly. "But that doesn't alter the fact that Dervish will last about five minutes if we leave him here."

"I'll be fine," Dervish growls.

"No," Beranabus says. "Your heart is finished. You'll die within days. That's not a guess," he adds as Dervish starts to argue. "And you wouldn't be able to do much during that time, apart from wheeze and clutch your chest a lot."

Dervish stares at the magician, jaw trembling. "It's really that bad?"

Beranabus nods soberly. "In the universe of magic, you might survive. Here, you're a dead man walking."

"Then get him there quick," Grubbs says. "I'll stay."

"Not you too," Beranabus groans. "What did I do to deserve as stubborn and reckless a pair as you?"

"It makes sense," Grubbs says, ignoring the cutting comment. "If the attacks were Lord Loss trying to get even, they're irrelevant. But if they're related to the Shadow, we need to know. I can confront the Lambs, find out if they're mixed up with the demon master, stop them if they are."

"Is the Shadow the creature we saw in the cave?" I ask, recalling the dark beast whom even Lord Loss seemed to be working for.

"Aye," Beranabus says. "We haven't learned much about it, except that it's put together an army of demons and is working hard to launch them across to our world." He studies Grubbs, frowning as he considers the teenager's proposal. "You'd operate alone?"

"I'd need help," Grubbs says. "Shark and Meera."

"I want to stay with Dervish," Meera says.

"He'll be fine," Grubbs overrules her. "He has Beranabus and Bec to look after him. Unless you want to leave Bec with me?" He raises an eyebrow.

"No," Beranabus mumbles. "If you're staying, I'll take her to replace you."

"Then go," Grubbs says. "Chase the truth on your side. I'll do the same here. If I discover no link between Lord Loss and the Lambs, I'll return. If they *are* working for him, I'll cull the whole bloody lot."

Kernel grunts, and a green window opens. "Time to decide," he tells Beranabus.

"Very well," the magician snaps. "But listen to Shark and Meera, heed their advice and contact me before you go running up against the likes of Lord Loss or the Shadow." He carefully picks up Sharmila and steps through the window with her. "Follow me, Bec."

I look around at the others, dazed by the speed with which things have been decided. Dervish is hugging Grubbs, squeezing him tightly, the way I wish he would have squeezed me all these long months.

"Are you OK with this?" Meera asks. "You don't want to stay?"

"I'll do what I must," I sigh.

"Take care of Dervish," Meera whispers.

"I will," I laugh, wishing I could remain with Meera instead of Dervish.

"Be wary," she croaks, dropping her voice even lower. "Beranabus has always been strongly driven, but he's almost insanely focused now. He says this Shadow he's been hunting is a massive threat to mankind, and he's determined to defeat it at all costs. But he's old and fuzzy-headed. He makes mistakes. Don't let him lead you astray."

"I'll keep an eye on him," I promise.

Dervish and Grubbs complete their farewells and the elder Grady stumbles through the window, rubbing the flesh around his chest, fighting back tears.

"Sorry we couldn't have more of a chat," Grubbs says to me.

"Next time." I smile.

"Yeah," he grunts skeptically. I can tell he thinks there will never be a time for simple chat. We belong to the world of pitched battle, and Grubbs believes we'll never escape it. I think he's right.

As Grubbs and Meera work their way across the roof to tell Shark about their new mission, I face Kernel Fleck. He's grinning at me sympathetically. "The world moves quickly when Beranabus is around," he says.

"What's it like through there?" I ask, nodding at the window.

"Bad." His grin slips. "The Shadow's promising the eradication of mankind and a new dawn of demon rule. Others have threatened that before, but the Shadow has convinced an army of demons — even powerful masters like Lord

Loss — that it can make good on its vow. We could be looking at the end this time." Kernel puts one foot into the panel of green light bridging two universes and beckons halfheartedly. "Let's go."

I take one last look at the human world — the night is bright with fires from the crashed helicopter and police searchlights — then wearily follow Kernel into the den of all things demonic.

CHASING SHADOWS

✠   ✠   ✠

WE'RE at an oasis in the middle of a desert. The trees are made out of bones, flaps of skin instead of leaves, and the well at the center is filled with a dark sulphurous liquid. The liquid's alive and can suck in and kill passers-by, but it only has a reach of two or three yards, so as long as we don't stray too close to it, we're safe.

The oasis was designed by a demon master a long time ago, based on something he'd seen on Earth. As much as demons hate humans and our world, they envy our forms and shapes. That's why many of them base their bodies on animals from our planet. They lack our imagination or the skills of Mother Nature.

We've been here for a week, although it's hard to judge the passage of time. There's one sun and moon above the oasis, like on Earth, but they never move. The sun shines for hours on end, holding its position in the sky, then abruptly dims to be replaced by the light of a three-quarters-full moon.

I haven't had to eat or drink since I came, and I've only

slept twice, a couple of hours each time. The magic in the air is far thicker than it was on my world sixteen hundred years ago. I could perform amazing feats here, turn a mountain upside down if I wanted. The trouble is, if I can do that much, so can the demons.

We haven't seen any of the Demonata yet. This is an abandoned region. Its master moved on or died, leaving only the skeletal trees and cannibalistic well. Individual demons wander through occasionally — some are picked off by the well — but incursions are rare. Beranabus has used it as a bolthole on several occasions.

Sharmila is still recovering, but we haven't been able to restore her lower legs. Magic works differently in each person. Kernel was able to replace his eyes when he lost them, but Sharmila can't grow new legs. You never know for sure what you can or can't do with your power until you test it.

Beranabus and I have used some of the bones and fleshy leaves from the trees to create artificial legs. We've attached them to Sharmila's thighs and she's spent the last couple of days adjusting, using magic to operate the limbs and keep her balance. She moves clumsily when she walks, and with great discomfort, but at least she's mobile. I don't know what will happen when she returns to the human world — the legs we've created won't work in a place without magic — but for now she's coping.

Dervish looks healthier too. I've taught him ways to direct magic into his heart, to strengthen and protect it. He should be fine as long as he stays here, but if he returns home the situation will rapidly change. His heart won't hold up long over there.

Dervish wove the material of his hospital gown in with scraps of flesh from the trees to create an outfit. He's also given himself a full head of silver hair and stuck it up in six long purple-tipped spikes. I was startled when I first saw it.

"I had spikes like this the last time I fought alongside Beranabus," he explained, blushing slightly. "I walked away alive then, so maybe they were good luck. We'll need all the luck we can muster when we fight again."

There's no doubt we'll have to fight either the Shadow or its army — or both. The first battles have already been waged. Before Meera and Shark tracked them down, Beranabus, Kernel, and Grubbs were flitting from realm to realm, hunting demons and challenging them, trying to find out more about the mysterious Shadow.

We saw the Shadow the night Bill-E was killed. A huge nebulous cloud of a monster, darker than any night, almost as black as the cave when I was sealed up there. Immensely powerful even by demonic standards.

Lord Loss said the creature would destroy humanity. The maudlin demon master craves human misery, feeding on it like a cat slurping milk. In my time he slyly helped me close a tunnel to stop a demon invasion. He needs humans the way a fish needs water.

But he's afraid of the Shadow. He doesn't believe mankind can defeat this new threat. He has sided with the creature, serving as if he was an ordinary demon, not a powerful master. He does the Shadow's bidding, even though that might mean the end of the human suffering he cherishes.

Lord Loss's fear of the Shadow fills Beranabus with unease. He believes the war between humanity and the

Demonata can't last forever. In the distant past, the powerful Old Creatures ruled the Earth and demons couldn't cross. By my time their power had waned. That led to the current war between humans and demons. Beranabus thinks we must find a way to block their passage between universes or they'll wipe us out completely.

The Kah-Gash has been Beranabus's only real hope. According to the ancient legends, the weapon can destroy a universe — ours or the Demonata's. He'd love to do that. It doesn't bother him that he'd be eradicating an entire life form. He sees this as a blood-drenched fight to the finish. The universes are colliding and only the victors will survive.

Beranabus has the Kah-Gash now — in the shape of Grubbs, Kernel, and me — but he doesn't trust it. The weapon has a will of its own. It worked through us when the world was last threatened by a demon breakthrough, but it's been silent since. We don't know what its plans or desires are.

Beranabus hoped to experiment, unlock the Kah-Gash's secrets, find out how to direct its great power. But so far he hasn't learned anything new.

Unwilling to unleash the Kah-Gash, Beranabus instead hunted for the shadowy monster we'd glimpsed in the cave. Having no name for it, he dubbed it the Shadow. The more he chased it, the more apt that name became.

Beranabus has interrogated many demons who know about the Shadow, but not one knows its real name. It's rumored to be more powerful than any other demon. They say it's been working in secrecy for hundreds of years. That it recently made itself known to a number of demon masters, recruiting them to help it achieve its ultimate aim — the removal of the human stain.

That's how demons see us, as a stain on the universes. They were here long before us and consider themselves superior. They hated the Old Creatures but respected them. They have nothing but contempt for our weak, mortal kind.

The Shadow has promised to kill every human and make the Demonata more powerful than ever. A few demons told Beranabus that it had even promised a return to the original state of the universes and the elimination of death, but we're not sure what that means. The demons weren't sure either.

Beranabus hasn't dared go after any of the masters. They're too powerful. He thinks the creature has made its base in Lord Loss's realm, but he dares not set foot there. And Kernel — who can usually find anything in either universe — isn't able to search for the beast since he doesn't know the thing's name and didn't see it in the cave, having been blind at the time. Beranabus has tried to magically re-create a picture of the Shadow, but it always comes up blurred and indistinct.

We spent the first couple of days here arguing about what to do next. While I worked tirelessly on Sharmila's legs — and helped her adjust to the shock when she regained consciousness — Dervish pressed Beranabus to focus on the werewolf and demon attacks.

"You've been chasing this Shadow for months without result," he argued. "This is something concrete, a puzzle we can solve. Better to direct our energies at a problem we can crack than waste them on an enigma."

"But all else is irrelevant," Beranabus bellowed. "The

Shadow is the greatest threat humanity has ever faced. We have to pursue it relentlessly, down as many blind alleys as it takes, until we find a demon who knows its name, where it comes from, how powerful it is. The knowledge is out there. We just have to find it. But we can't do that if we squander our time on a bunch of hairy Grady miscreants!"

Dervish countered by insisting the attacks were linked to the Shadow. We know Lord Loss is working for him, and that the revived Juni Swan works for Lord Loss.

"Maybe Lord Loss and Juni just want to kill us before the world is ruined," he said. "But they might be planning to use the werewolves to target the Disciples, kill as many as they can and clear the way for crossings."

Kernel supported Dervish. "We can't go after Lord Loss directly — he's too powerful," he said. "But we can target Juni. Lord Loss didn't show himself at the hospital, but Juni was acting on his behalf. She might have been part of the group in Carcery Vale too. If more assaults on the Disciples are planned, she'll possibly act as the go-between again, conveying Lord Loss's orders to their allies. If we can trap her, we can find out what she knows about the Shadow."

Beranabus was swayed by that and told Kernel to devote himself to tracking her movements. I think he's keen to get his hands on Juni for personal reasons. She betrayed him. But it's not just revenge he's interested in. He also wants to know how she came back.

We don't understand how my soul remained trapped in the cave when I died, or how I returned to life. That's never happened before. Ghosts exist, but they're mere after-images of people. We don't know where a person's soul goes when they die — if there's a heavenly realm, if they get re-born, or if they simply cease to exist. But they always move on. Never, in all of history, has a person's soul survived death and returned to life. Until me. And now Juni.

Beranabus believes I survived because I'm part of the Kah-Gash. The mystical weapon turned back time, so it could feasibly cheat death too. But Juni isn't a piece of the Kah-Gash. She shouldn't have been able to survive the destruction of her body. Her return troubles Beranabus deeply. He suspects it's linked to the rise of the Shadow. If the new demon leader has the power to restore life, maybe it shares other powers in common with the Kah-Gash. Beranabus wants — *needs* — to know.

So Kernel has been focusing on Juni and Lord Loss for the last few days. He's developed in many ways since the three of us worked in league as the Kah-Gash. He can do more than open windows now. He can search for several people at the same time and track their movements — he knows when they switch from one realm or universe to the other.

Juni is currently in Lord Loss's kingdom, with her master. But as soon as she moves, Kernel will know and we'll blaze into action.

✠ I've spent a lot of time with Beranabus. He's changed so much over the centuries, made himself hard and uncaring, believing he had to be like a demon in order to fight the Demonata. It helped that he is half-demon. There's a monster within him, always active, struggling to rise to the surface. Beranabus has to fight it constantly to maintain control, but through those battles he's learned more about demons and their ways than he ever could have otherwise.

One of his greatest fears is that he'll go insane and the demon within him will take over. It would be the ultimate irony — the man who spent all his life battling to save humans from the Demonata turns into one of them and goes on a massive killing spree.

Beranabus can discuss such fears with me because I already know about them. I absorbed his secrets along with his memories, so he can't hide them from me. I know almost as much about the ancient magician as he does.

"Sometimes I wonder if my life's been worthwhile," he muttered last night when we were apart from the others. "I've gone without pleasure or company for most of my years. If we lose and the Demonata kill us all, there won't have been a point. Maybe I should have settled, married, had children, lived a normal life. It might not have made any difference in the end."

I tried to make him see that millions of people owe their lives to him, that the Demonata would have taken over our world many centuries before this if not for his stubborn resistance. But he's fallen into a dark state of mind. I think partly it's because of my return. I've made him aware of all that he's missed out on. If he'd allowed himself to be more human, he'd have had friends and family, and perhaps been much happier.

I'm sitting beneath the shade of a bony tree, trying to think of a way to ease Beranabus's troubled mind. Someone coughs close by, disturbing me. I open my eyes and find Dervish standing there. "Mind if I sit down?"

I nudge over. When he's sitting, he smiles awkwardly. We

haven't said much to each other since he recovered. I think he's embarrassed — we'd had that big conversation prior to the attacks, but never had a chance to wrap it up.

"How are you getting on?" he asks.

"Not too bad."

"It's pretty boring here, huh?"

I shrug. "I'd rather this to the excitement of fighting demons."

He strokes one of his newly grown spikes. "What do you think of the hair?"

"Some of the warriors in my time styled their hair like that," I tell him.

"Yeah?" He looks proud.

"But they were all a lot younger than you."

He makes a face. "I started going bald early, so I had no choice other than adapt. But I never liked looking like the crown of an egg."

"Baldness suits old men."

"I'm not . . ." He starts to protest, then sighs. "No, you're right, I *am* old. It happened while I wasn't looking. Old, bald, dodgy heart, ignorant."

"Ignorant?" I echo.

"The way I treated you," he says softly. "I was an ignorant old man. If Billy or Grubbs had seen me acting that way, they'd have kicked me hard and told me to stop being an idiot."

"You were upset," I excuse him. "People do strange things when they lose a loved one."

"I should have known better," he grunts. "I would have been more sensitive a few years ago, but you don't see things so clearly when you let yourself become a grumpy old fogey. I used to criticise Ma and Pa Spleen — Billy's grandparents — for being cranky and small-minded. But I was turning into a carbon copy of them." He shudders.

"Bill-E loved his grandparents regardless of their flaws," I say. "He would have gone on loving and forgiving you too, no matter what."

"How about you?" Dervish asks.

I frown uncomfortably. I should say something diplomatic, but I was reared to speak my mind. "I don't love you. I hardly even know you."

"I didn't mean that," Dervish says quickly. "I meant, can you forgive me? Can we be friends? Or will I always be the ogre who made you tell him stories about a dead boy for months on end?"

"You'll always be an ogre," I say seriously, then laugh at his expression. "I'm joking. Of course we can be friends."

"We can start over?" he says eagerly. "Get to know each other properly?"

I nod, and he sticks out a hand to shake on the deal.

"You know about my gift?" I say hesitantly.

"Yes. But I don't care. You don't hold things back from friends."

I smile, then shyly shake his cool, wrinkled, welcome hand.

✠ Kernel is off by himself, doggedly monitoring Juni's position. The rest of us are dueling, practicing our skills, learning. It's difficult to define your magical limits. Magic is a mysterious, ever-shifting force. You can test yourself in certain ways on Earth, but you never know how far you can stretch until circumstances compel you to improvize.

Sharmila told me that when Kernel first came to this universe, Beranabus threw him at a flesh-eating tree to establish his magical potential. When his life came under threat, Kernel reacted and he fought free. If he'd been of lesser potential, he'd have perished. That's a cruel way to test a person, but there's no easy alternative. Magic is part of a harsh universe. Those who wish to channel its power must accept that.

Beranabus sends twin balls of fire shooting at Dervish and me. I turn the ball aimed at me into an icy mist, but Dervish isn't as swift. He disperses the flames, but not before they singe his beard and redden his cheeks and lips.

"You're slow," Beranabus grunts while Dervish repairs the damage.

"So are you!" Sharmila shouts, hitting Beranabus with a burst of energy from behind. He shoots forward, yelling with surprise, and smashes into a tree, sending bones flying in all directions.

"That hurt," Beranabus complains, staggering to his feet and rubbing the small of his back. He bends to pick some splinters out of his bare feet. We've all gotten rid of our shoes — they hinder the flow of magic.

"Be thankful I was not aiming to kill," Sharmila says coolly. "We are all slower and weaker than before. It is the penalty of old age. No one can avoid it."

"I've done better than most for a millennium and a half," Beranabus growls.

"But time catches up with us all eventually, even you."

Beranabus twists slowly left, then right, working the pain out of his back. "I suppose you're right," he grumbles. "I've known for a long time I'm not as quick or powerful as I once was."

He waves a hand at Sharmila, and her artificial legs snap apart. She collapses with a yelp of shock and pain.

"But there's life in the old dog yet," Beranabus shouts triumphantly before guiltily hurrying to Sharmila's side to fix the damage.

✠ Kernel has kept himself distant, sitting in the open with his legs crossed, tinkering with the lights that only he can see, keeping tabs on Juni. Beranabus told me his bald assistant finds it hard to focus these days. Since he got his new eyes he's been seeing patches of light that were invisible to him before. He can't control the new patches and they distract him. He's been trying to ignore them, but I often spot him scowling and cursing, waving an irritated hand at the air around him.

In the middle of another dry, lifeless afternoon, as the others are resting while I leap from tree to tree testing my powers of flight, Kernel uncrosses his legs and stands.

"She's moving," he says.

We're by his side in seconds. His bright blue eyes are alive with flickering spots of light. He looks nervous.

"Where did she go?" Beranabus asks.

"Earth."

"And Lord Loss?"

"He stayed in his own realm."

"Can you tell where exactly she is?" Dervish asks.

"No." He frowns. "I should be able to, but I can't place it."

"Is she close to Grubbs?" Dervish presses.

Kernel concentrates, then shakes his head.

"Well?" Sharmila asks Beranabus.

"Kernel and I will investigate. The rest of you stay here."

"Nuts to that," Dervish huffs.

"Don't forget about your heart," Beranabus says. "Or Sharmila's legs. You're a pair of wrecks on that world. Let us check the situation and report back. We won't engage her if we can avoid it."

"What about me?" I ask. "I can survive there."

"Aye, but I'm asking you to wait. Please. Until we know more about what we're walking into."

I don't like it, but I know Beranabus worries about me. Better to go along with his wishes, so he can operate free of any distractions.

Kernel opens a window within minutes. It's a white panel of light. I think I can smell the real world through it, but that's just my nose playing tricks. Without saying anything, Kernel steps through, Beranabus half a step behind him.

"We'll give them five minutes," Dervish rumbles. "If they're not back by then, we —"

Beranabus sticks his head through the window, catching us by surprise. "It's an area of magic," he says. "Sharmila and Dervish will be fine there. Come on."

He disappears again. We glance at each other uneasily, then file through one by one, back to the human universe, in search of the semi-human Juni Swan and a host of shadowy answers.

PART THREE

✠ ✠ ✠

ALL ABOARD

SNAPSHOTS OF BERANABUS III

✠   ✠   ✠

BERANABUS *thought his world had ended when I died. He'd been developing while we were together, the disjointed fragments of his mind linking up, learning to think and reason as other humans did. My magic helped. Unknown to me, I smoothed out many of the creases inside his brain, opening channels that had been blocked. Perhaps, deep down, I loved him as he loved me. I was certainly fond of the strange boy.*

When the rocks closed, trapping me in the cave with Lord Loss and his familiars, Beranabus went wild with grief. He tried to carve through the wall, using small stones and his bare fingers. When that failed, he kept vigil for several months, drinking from the waterfall inside the cave, abandoning his post only to catch the occasional rabbit or fox.

He held long, garbled conversations with himself in the darkness. Time got confused inside his head, and sometimes he thought he was in the Labyrinth and the Minotaur was hiding behind a stalagmite. He'd repeat my name over and over, along with his own — he managed to say "Beranabus" for the first time in the cave. He wept and howled, and sometimes tried to bash his head open on the rocks. Normally he stopped before damaging himself, but a few times he knocked himself unconscious, only to awake hours later, scalp bruised and bloody, his ears ringing.

He knew I was dead, that the rock wouldn't open, that I'd never step out and throw my arms around him. But for a long time he clung to the belief that a miracle would return me to the world. Then, one day, without warning, he kissed the rock, climbed to the surface, and staggered away, with no intention of ever coming back.

✠ Beranabus retraced our steps, following the route we'd covered from the shoreline to the cave. He hoped, by doing so, to recall any small memories of me that he might have forgotten. His vague plan was to march west to the shore, then back inland to the crannog where I'd first met Drust, finishing up at my village. After that . . . he didn't know. Thinking ahead was a new experience for him, and he found it hard to look very far into the future.

When he reached the shore and gazed down over the cliff where we'd sheltered, to the ever-angry sea below, his plan changed. Grief exploded within him and he saw only one way to escape it. He'd had enough of demons and humans, slaughter and love. He didn't know much about death, but the many corpses he'd seen over the centuries had all looked peaceful and unthinking. Maybe he wouldn't feel this terrible sense of loss if he put life and its complicated emotions behind him.

Beranabus smiled as he stepped off the cliff and fell. His

thoughts were of me and the Minotaur. He knew nothing of the possibility of a life after death, so he had no hope of seeing us again. His only wish was that our faces were the last images in his thoughts when he died.

The water was colder than he expected, and he shouted with alarm when he hit. But as he sank into the new subterranean world, he relaxed. The cold wasn't so bad after a while, and though he didn't like the way the salt water washed down his throat, he'd experienced more unpleasant sensations in the universe of the Demonata.

That should have been the end of him, an anonymous, pointless death as Theseus had predicted so many centuries before. But beings of ancient, mysterious magic dwelt nearby, and they were watching. Known to humans as the Old Creatures, they'd once controlled the world. Now they were dying, or had moved on, and only a few were left.

Some of them lived in a cave beneath the cliff from which Beranabus had jumped — they were the reason Drust had gone there in the first place. They sensed the boy's peculiar brand of magic and curiously probed the corridors of his mind. The Old Creatures took an interest in the drowning boy and instead of letting him drift out to sea and a welcome death, they drew him to the cave against his will. He washed up on the floor, where he reluctantly spat out water and instinctively gasped for air, even though he would rather have suffocated.

When Beranabus could speak, he roared at the pillars of light (the Old Creatures had no physical bodies). He knew they'd saved him and he hated them for it. He cursed gibberish, trying to make them explain why they hadn't let him die.

"We Have Need Of You," the Old Creatures answered, the words forming inside the boy's brain. "You May Be Able To Help Us."

Beranabus roared at them again, and although he couldn't express his feelings verbally, the Old Creatures knew what he wanted to say.

"Yes, She Is Dead, But Her Soul Has Not Departed This World. She Can Return To You." Beranabus squinted at the shifting lights. "If You Remain With Us, Let Us Teach And Direct You, And Serve As We Wish, You Will Meet Your Bec Again."

The promise captivated Beranabus and filled his heart with warmth and hope. It didn't cross his mind that the Old Creatures could be lying, and he never wondered what they might ask of him. They'd said he'd see his young love again — that was all that mattered. Putting dark thoughts and longings for death behind him, he presented himself to the formless Old Creatures and awaited their bidding, leaving them free to mold and do with him as they wished.

✠ Beranabus could never remember much of his time with the Old Creatures, even though he spent more than a century in the cavern. They taught him to speak and reason, completing his evolution from confused child to intelligent young adult.

As his intellect developed, he came to believe that the Old Creatures had lied about my return. He didn't blame them — he knew it was the only way they could have calmed and controlled him. He had accepted my death and moved on. He was older and wiser, tougher than he'd been as a child, and although he still loved and mourned me, he had other issues to focus on. He had demons to kill.

Beranabus hated the Demonata — they'd slaughtered his beloved — and the Old Creatures encouraged this hatred. They showed him how to open windows to the demon universe and explained how he could channel magic to kill the beasts. They sent him on his first missions, directing him to specific spots, targeting vulnerable demons.

Beranabus never questioned their motives. He assumed that everyone on this world hated the demons as much as he did, even though the Old Creatures were not of the human realm and seemed to be under no threat. They were more powerful — in this universe at least — than the Demonata, so they had nothing to fear from them.

As he developed a taste for killing, Beranabus spent more and more time in the demon universe, using the cave of the Old Creatures as a base that he visited rarely, when he needed to sleep, treat his wounds, and recover.

✚ One night, after an especially long spell butchering demons, he returned to the cave and the Old Creatures were gone. He would have known it even if he was blind. The magic had faded from the air and it now felt like a cold, dead place.

In a panic, Beranabus scaled the cliff from which he'd hurled himself many decades before and searched frantically for the Old Creatures. He found traces of them in a place called Newgrange. Druids had claimed the celestial dome and worshipped and studied the stars from there. But it had been built by the Old Creatures, who used it as a navigational point when traveling between worlds.

One of the Old Creatures was waiting in the gloom of the dome for Beranabus. It took the form of a small ball of swirling light, less grand than any of the pillars had been in the cave.

"It Is Time For Us To Go," the Old Creature said. "We Must Leave This Planet."

Beranabus went cold. Without the protective magic of the Old Creatures, the world would be at the mercy of the Demonata.

"You're abandoning us!" Beranabus cried angrily.

"We Are Leaving," the Old Creature agreed, "But We Have Left You In Our Place. You Must Guard This World Now."

"I can't protect humanity by myself," Beranabus exploded. "I can't be everywhere at once, stop every crossing or kill every demon who makes it through."

"No," the Old Creature said calmly, "But You Can Try."

"Why?" Beranabus groaned. "Why desert us now, when we need you most?"

"Our Time Has Passed," the Old Creature said. "You People Must Fend For Yourselves Or Perish. We Cannot Protect You Forever." As Beranabus started to argue, the Old Creature hushed him. "We Have One Last Thing To Tell You, One Final Mission To Send You On."

"I won't be your servant any longer," Beranabus snarled, tears of rage hot in his eyes.

"There Was A Force Once, A Weapon Of Sorts," the Old Creature said, ignoring his protest. "The Kah-Gash. It Shattered Into A Number Of Pieces That Have Been Lost Ever Since. You Must Search For Those Fragments And Reunite Them."

"I don't understand," Beranabus said, intrigued despite his bitter fury.

"The Kah-Gash Can Be Used To Destroy An Entire Universe. If The Demonata Find The Pieces And Assemble Them, They Can Annihilate This Universe And Remove Every Last Trace Of Mankind. But If You Find Them . . ."

". . . I can destroy their universe!" Beranabus exclaimed.

"Perhaps," the Old Creature said. And then it was gone, the ball of light shooting through the hole in the roof, streaking towards the stars, not even bidding Beranabus farewell.

Beranabus had a hundred questions he wanted answered, but there was no one to ask. He could feel the loss of the Old Creatures in the air. They'd left artifacts behind — lodestones charged with powerful Old Magic — but their influence would fade with time, opening the way for more demon attacks.

He had to act quickly. The Old Creature hadn't said as much, but Beranabus assumed there were demons looking for the Kah-Gash, and he would have to race against them to find the missing pieces. It occurred to him that the demons might have been searching for millions of years, but that didn't deter him. He was arrogant. He believed he would succeed where the Demonata had failed, find the weapon, and deliver the ultimate blow.

Setting off through the countryside, he steeled himself for what was to come. He sensed it wouldn't be easy, that it might take centuries — or longer — to locate all the pieces. But he would triumph eventually. Nothing could stand in his way. In his youthful arrogance he believed this was his destiny and that if he needed more time to complete his mission, he could even defy death if he had to.

KIRILLI

I step through the window and find myself on a highly polished wooden floor. There are no walls or ceiling, only a clear blue sky and glaring sun far overhead. I squint and cover my eyes with a hand. When my pupils adjust, I slowly lower my hand and stare around with awe.

We're surrounded by water — we must be on a boat. Everywhere I look, an ocean stretches ahead of me, small waves lazily rippling by. I've only seen the sea once before, and that was from the safety of land. Finding myself stranded in the middle of it makes me feel sick. Even though the floor is steady, my legs seem to wobble beneath me and I have to fight to calm my stomach.

"Easy, Little One," Beranabus murmurs, touching my arm and smiling.

"It's so vast," I whisper, eyes round.

"Aye, but it's only the sea. You've nothing to fear."

"But the monsters . . ." I catch myself. In my time we

thought the sea was home to an array of terrors. Now I know that isn't so. I remind myself that I'm not living in the fifth century any longer. Frowning at myself for overreacting, I order my legs to steady and my stomach to stop churning.

Breathing more calmly, I pivot slowly and study the vessel on which we've landed. We're on the deck of a massive ship, a luxury cruise liner, but its grandeurs have been spoiled by a recent vicious attack. Deck chairs are strewn everywhere. We're close to a swimming pool — the water is red and there are bodies floating in it. A man lies spread-eagled on a diving board, blood dripping from his throat into the water. More corpses dot the deck and some are draped over deck chairs.

There are carcasses everywhere. Freshly dead, with blood oozing from them. Men, women, and children. Some are in crew uniforms, others in swimwear or casual clothes. Apart from the soft dripping noises of the blood, there's no sound, not even the chug of an engine. The boat is as dead as the butchered passengers and staff.

As I gaze with horror at the carnage, the more experienced Sharmila checks a few of the bodies to ensure they're beyond help. "Juni could not have killed all these people by herself," she says quietly.

"She could," Beranabus grunts, "but I don't think she did. You can see different marks if you look closely. A group of demons had a party here."

"Where are they now?" Dervish asks, fingers flexing angrily.

"That's what I'd like to know." Beranabus walks to the diving board, steps on to it, and pushes the body off into the water as if it was a rubbish bag — he can be as detached as a demon when he needs to be. The splash disturbs the silence. We wait edgily, but nothing reacts to the noise.

"Are you sure Dervish and Sharmila are safe here?" I ask Kernel, trying to find something other than the corpses to focus on. "There's magic in the air, but I'm not sure it will hold."

"It's secure," he assures me. "We wouldn't have brought them over if we had any doubts. We're surrounded by a bubble of magical energy. The entire ship's been encased."

"Like the town of Slawter," Dervish notes, then tugs anxiously at his beard. "This bubble — it's pretty impenetrable?"

"Yes," Kernel says.

"So if the window to the oasis blinks out of existence, we're trapped."

Kernel smiles. "Don't worry. I'll keep it open. That's what I excel at."

Beranabus returns from the diving board. "They must have a lodestone on board. No demon could maintain a shield like this without a lodestone."

Lodestones are stones of ancient — Old — power. Demons can use them to seal off an area and fill it with magic. That lets them operate as if they were in their own universe. They can use them to open tunnels as well, if the stone is especially powerful. But they need human help. They can't do it alone.

Lodestones are rare. When the Old Creatures inhabited the Earth, they used the stones to help keep back the Demonata. But in their absence the demons learned to turn the magic of the stones against the humans they were originally intended to protect. Beranabus scoured the world for lodestones centuries ago and destroyed as many as he could find, or sealed them off like the one in Carcery Vale. But some evaded him and remain hidden in various corners of the world. Every so often a mage or demon tracks one down and trouble ensues.

"Is Juni still here?" Dervish asks Kernel.

"Yes," I answer first. "I sense her near the bottom of the ship."

"This feels like a trap," Sharmila mutters.

"Aye," Beranabus says. "But you learn to live with traps when you're chasing demons." He looks around. "Are there any others, Bec?"

I let my senses drift through the areas below deck. "There's one demon with Juni. Not very powerful. If there are others, they're masking themselves."

"There's a window open down there," Kernel says. "Fairly ordinary. Only weaker demons can cross through it."

"Could there be armed humans?" Dervish asks.

"Perhaps," I mutter. "Humans are harder to sense than mages or demons."

"We can handle a few soldiers," Beranabus barks. "I'll turn their guns into eels — see how much damage they can do with them then!"

"We should go back," Sharmila says. "Juni has set this up to ensnare us."

"Why would she be expecting us?" Dervish argues.

"Lord Loss may have reasoned that we would target Juni. Perhaps everything — the attacks on Dervish, Juni revealing herself on the roof of the hospital — was designed to lure Beranabus here. The demon master might be poised to cross and finish us off personally."

"Not through that window," Kernel insists.

"Then through another," she counters. "We have never been able to explain why Lord Loss can cross when other masters cannot, or how he goes about it."

Beranabus considers that, then sighs. "You could be right, but we might never get a better shot at Juni. If she's not expecting us, it's the perfect time to strike. If she is and this is a trap, at least we can anticipate the worst. The magic in the air means she'll be dangerous, but it serves us as much as her. If Lord Loss doesn't turn up, we can match her. If he does cross, we'll make a swift getaway."

"Are you sure of that?" Sharmila scowls. "If we have to open a new window —"

"We won't," Beranabus says. "Kernel will stay here and guard our escape route. You'll know if any other windows open, won't you?"

"Yes," Kernel says.

"Then keep this one alive and watch for signs of further activity. If you sense anything, summon us and we'll withdraw. Is everyone satisfied with that?" He looks pointedly at Sharmila. She frowns, then shrugs. Taking the lead, Beranabus picks his way across the bloody, corpse-strewn deck, and the rest of us cautiously, nervously follow.

✠ My feet are soon sticky with blood, but I ignore my queasy feelings. This isn't the way the world should be, having to creep through pools of blood, past dozens of slaughtered humans. But when you find yourself in the middle of a living nightmare you have two choices. You can cower in a corner, eyes shut, praying for it to be over. Or you can get on with things and do your best to deal with the job at hand. I don't think I'm particularly brave, but I like to think I've always been practical.

We undertake a circuit of the upper deck before venturing into the depths of the ship, making sure there aren't any surprises waiting for us up here if we have to make a quick getaway. We don't find any demons or soldiers in league with the Demonata. Just one corpse after another, slowly frying beneath the merciless sun.

We're passing a row of lifeboats when I feel a twitch at the back of my eyes. It's the subtlest of sensations. I'd ignore it any other time. But I'm trying to be alert to the least hint of anything amiss, so I stop and focus. The twitch draws me to the third boat ahead of us. It hangs from hooks high above the deck.

"What is it?" Beranabus whispers. I feel magic build within him. He's converting the energy in the air into a force he can use.

"Somebody's there." I point to the lifeboat. "A man. Hiding from us. He's using a masking spell."

"Get ready," Beranabus says to the others. He points a finger at the hooks. They snap and the boat drops abruptly, landing hard on the deck. The man inside it yelps and tumbles out as the boat keels over.

Sharmila and Dervish step ahead of Beranabus, fingers crackling with pent-up magic. The man shrieks and wildly raises his hands, shouting, "I surrender!"

"Wait!" Sharmila snaps, grabbing Dervish's arm. "I know him."

The man pauses when he hears Sharmila's voice. He stares at her shakily, as if he doesn't believe his ears or eyes.

"Kirilli Kovacs," Sharmila says.

"I . . . I recognize you . . . I think," he croaks.

"We met several years ago. You were with Zahava Lever. She was your mentor. My name is Sharmila —"

"— Mukherji," the man says, breaking into a big smile. "Of course. Zavi spoke very highly of you. She said you were a great Disciple, one of the finest. I should have recognized you immediately. My apologies. It's been a hard few . . ." He frowns. "I was going to say days, but it's only been hours."

"This is one of your lot?" Beranabus sniffs. We're all a bit mystified. The man is wearing a dark suit, but there are silver and gold stars stitched into the shoulders and down the sides. He sports a thin moustache and is wearing mascara. He looks like a stage magician, not a Disciple.

"This is my cover," he explains sheepishly. "I ran into fiscal complications. . . ." He clears his throat. "Actually I gambled away my cash and my credit card was taken from me by a woman in . . . but that's another story. I had to get on the ship. I could have used magic but it was easier to get a job. So I did, as Kirilli the Konjuror. I've used this disguise before. It's always been effective. I can put on a first-rate stage show when I have to."

"Your standards are slipping," Beranabus says to Sharmila. "I might have to review the recruiting policy of the Disciples."

"I'm of a first-rate pedigree, sir," Kirilli snaps. "Even the best of us can fall prey to the occasional vice." He tugs the arms of his jacket straight and glares.

"Zahava said Kirilli was an excellent spy," Sharmila says. "He is very adept at trailing people and hiding from them. The fact that he survived the massacre here is proof of that. The Disciples need spies as much as they need warriors."

"Precisely," Kirilli huffs. "There's a man for every job, as my dear departed father used to say."

"I bet he worked in sewage," Dervish says drily.

Kirilli flushes but ignores the jibe. "By the way," he says stiffly, "I didn't catch *your* names."

Beranabus shrugs. "This is Dervish Grady. That's Bec. I'm Beranabus."

Kirilli's jaw drops and he loses his composure completely.

Beranabus winks at me. "I have that effect on a lot of my idolizing Disciples."

"Only until we get to know you," Sharmila mutters, then addresses Kirilli again. "Can you tell us what happened? Swiftly, please — we do not have much time."

"That's really Beranabus?" Kirilli says, wide-eyed. "I thought he'd look more like Merlin or Gandalf."

"He'll turn you into a hobbit if you don't start talking," Dervish growls.

Kirilli blanches, then scowls. "I was tracking a pair of rogue mages," he says, adjusting his bowtie — I spot a playing card up his sleeve. "They were planning to open a window."

"Why didn't you stop them?" Dervish asks.

"They were working for somebody else, taking orders

from a superior. I wanted to expose their partner. I felt that was more important than stopping the crossing, although I'd hoped to do that as well."

"No prizes for guessing who their boss was." Dervish grimaces. "Ugly cow, disfigured, covered in pus and blood?"

Kirilli nods and shivers. "They were in regular contact, but I couldn't get a fix on who they were talking to. From what I overheard, it sounded like there were no imminent plans to open the window. They made it sound like they'd be on the boat for months, waiting for an order to act.

"They either knew I was eavesdropping and said that to fool me, or there was a change of plan. Either way, they opened the window earlier today. About twenty demons spat through and set to work on the crew and guests. I managed to shield myself. That's all I could do. There was no point fighting them — I wouldn't have stood a chance." He looks at us appealingly.

"You did all you could," Sharmila says kindly. "You are a spy, not a warrior. Besides, Disciples never fight when the odds are stacked against them. You have no reason to feel guilty."

Gratitude sweeps across Kirilli's face. "I expected the window to close after a few minutes but it stayed open and there was more magic in the air than I've ever experienced. The demons went on torturing and slaughtering. They took most of the people below deck. Maybe the sun bothered them and they wanted to do their work in the shade."

"No," Beranabus grunts. "Lodestones need blood. They were feeding it."

"What's a lodestone?" Kirilli asks, but Beranabus waves at

him to continue. "Balint and Zsolt — the mages — remained up top. They did their share of killing but nothing to compare with the demons. Not long before you lot arrived that woman . . . that *thing* . . . crawled up from below." He shudders. "I wasn't sure if she was human or Demonata. I'm still not certain."

"I doubt if she knows herself anymore," Beranabus says softly.

"She barked orders at the demons, and they killed the last few survivors," Kirilli goes on. "Then they retreated through the window and the woman said a spell to close it. Balint and Zsolt were grinning, mightily pleased with themselves, but she turned on them. Melted them into twin pools of bloody goo. Laughed as they screamed for mercy. Told them they were fools to trust the word of a monster. She lay down and wallowed in their juices when they were dead, then went below deck. That's when I climbed into the lifeboat."

"Interesting," Beranabus murmurs. Then he winks at Sharmila. "This definitely stinks of a trap."

"So we will leave?" Sharmila asks eagerly.

Beranabus chuckles. "I've walked into more traps over the centuries than I can remember. The Demonata and their familiars think they're masters of cunning, but they haven't got the better of me yet. Let Juni and Lord Loss spring their surprise. I'll blast a hole in it so big, you could sail this ship through."

"Are you sure?" Dervish asks uneasily. "Juni was your apprentice. She knows all about you. Maybe you have a weak spot that she plans to exploit."

Beranabus shrugs. "I love a challenge."

"I really do not think we should —" Sharmila begins.

"We've no choice," Beranabus snaps. "She's our only link to the Shadow. It's a gamble, but this is a time for gambling. I don't think you understand the stakes. This is the end-game. We don't have the luxury of caution. If we don't risk all and find out who the Shadow is and what its plans are, the world will fall." He waves at the corpses around us. "A world of *this*, Sharmila. Is that what you want?"

"Of course not," she mutters.

"Then trust me. We're precariously balanced, and I might be testing one trap too many, but we can't play safe. It's all or nothing now."

"You truly believe matters are that advanced?" Sharmila asks.

"Aye." Beranabus's eyes glitter. "The Disciples have exercised caution over the years because there have always been other battles to fight. But this could be the final battle. Ever. Better to risk all on a desperate gamble than play it safe and hand victory to the Shadow. Aye?"

Sharmila hesitates, then smiles shakily. "*Aye.* If we fail, at least I will have the pleasure of saying, 'I told you so.'"

"That's the spirit," Beranabus booms and heads for the nearest door. Without any sign of fear he leads us down into the bowels of the ship in search of the vile viper, Juni Swan.

HER MASTER'S VOICE

✠ ✠ ✠

We progress in single file, Beranabus leading, Sharmila second, then me and Kirilli, with Dervish bringing up the rear. As we start down the first set of steps, Kirilli whispers, "Care to let me know what's going on? I caught some of it, but I'm in the dark on a lot of issues."

"There's a powerful new demon called the Shadow," I explain. "We need to find out more about it. Juni — the mutant you saw — possesses information."

"And all that talk of a trap . . . ?"

"We think Juni or Lord Loss may have lured us here, that they might be trying to trap us. This could all be a setup."

"The plot thickens," Kirilli says, trying to sound lighthearted but failing to hide the squeak in his voice. "Any idea what the odds are? I'm a gambling man, so I knew where Beranabus was coming from when I heard him talking about the need to take risks. But I like to have an idea of the odds before I place a bet."

"We honestly don't know," I tell him.

He makes a humming noise. "Let's say two-to-one. Those are fair odds. I've bet on a lot worse in my time."

He's trembling. This is a new level for him. The wholesale slaughter on the deck shook him up and now he's being asked to disregard Disciple protocol — run when the odds are against you — and fight to a very probable death.

"You don't need to come with us," I murmur. "We left someone up top to keep our escape route open. You could wait with him."

Kirilli smiles nervously. "I'd love to, but I've always dreamed of standing beside the legendary Beranabus in battle. I was never this scared in my dreams, but if I back out now I won't be able to forgive myself."

We start down a long corridor. There are bodies lying in tattered, bloodied bundles at regular intervals. I wonder how many people a ship this size holds. Three thousand? Four? I've never heard the death screams of thousands of people. The noise must have been horrible.

"Have you fought before?" I ask Kirilli, to distract myself.

"Not really," he says. "As Sharmila said, I'm a spy. Excellent at sniffing out intrigue and foiling the well-laid plans of villainous rogues like Zsolt and Balint. But when it comes to the dirty business of killing, I'm more a stabber in the back than a face-to-face man. Never saw anything wrong with striking an opponent from behind if they're a nasty piece of work."

"I doubt if Juni will turn her back on you. The best thing is to trust in your magic and try not to think too much. If you're attacked, use your instincts. You'll find yourself doing things you never thought possible."

"And if my instincts come up short?" Kirilli asks.

Dervish snorts behind us. "That'll be a good time to panic."

Kirilli frowns over his shoulder at Dervish. "It's rude to eavesdrop."

"I'm a rude kind of guy," Dervish retorts. "Don't worry, you'll be fine. Hang back when we get there, fire off the occasional bolt of energy — at our opponents, not us — and try not to get in anyone's way."

"I can tell you're a true leader of men," Kirilli says sarcastically.

"Quiet," Beranabus snarls. "I'm trying to concentrate."

"Sorry, boss," Dervish says, then sticks his right hand under his left armpit and makes a farting noise. We all giggle, even Beranabus. It's not unnatural to laugh in the face of death. It's not an act of bravery either. You do it because you might never have the chance to laugh again.

✠ We descend slowly, exploring each level, wary of booby traps. But there are no secret windows, no army of demons, no humans packing weapons.

We pass a mound of bodies, mostly uniformed crew. They armed themselves with axes, knives, flares — whatever they could find — and tried to block off the corridor with bulky pieces of furniture. The demons ripped through them. They never stood a chance.

The lights suddenly snap off. Kirilli gasps and grabs my hand. I get images of his previous limited encounters with demons, his stage act, the tricks he performs. He wanted to be a famous magician when he was young. Practiced hard, but didn't have the style. Good enough for clubs and cruises, but he never had a real crack at the big time. He was pleased when he joined the Disciples, proud of his talent. But he'd have much rather succeeded in showbiz, where the worst he'd have ever had to face was being booed offstage.

Emergency lights flicker on. There's a harsh metallic ripping sound somewhere far below. It echoes through the ship. The floor shudders, then steadies.

"Turbulence?" Beranabus asks.

"You only get that on planes," Dervish says. "It could be the roll of the sea, but I doubt it. Have you noticed the lack of movement? We haven't tilted since we came aboard. The ship's been steady, held in place by magic."

"I knew there was something strange," Kirilli growls. "I get terrible seasickness. I have to take pills to keep my food down. But I've been feeling fine for the last few hours. I thought I'd found my sea legs at last."

The ripping noise comes again, louder than before. It reminds me of a noise Bill-E heard in a film about the *Titanic,* when the iceberg sliced through the hull and split it open.

"Any idea what's going on down there?" Dervish asks.

Beranabus shrugs. "We'll soon find out."

We press on.

✠ Eventually we hit the bottom of the ship. Except there isn't much left of it. When we step into the cavernous hold, we instantly see what the noises were. The lowest layer has been peeled away. A huge hole has been gouged out of the hull, eighty or a hundred feet wide, stretching far ahead of us, through the middle of the hold and up the walls at the sides. Water surrounds the gap, held back by a field of magic. If that field was to suddenly collapse, the sea would flood through and the ship would sink swiftly.

There are bodies all over the place, but a huge pile is stacked in the center of the floorless hold, resting in a heap on the invisible barrier. It looks like they're floating on air.

The tip of a large stone juts through the covering of corpses. Red streaks of blood line the cracks and indentations of the ancient stone. The bodies around it are pale and shriveled. The stone has drunk from them. I recall the stone in the cave where I was imprisoned, when I sacrificed Drust, how it sucked his blood. These stones of magic are alive in some way. The Old Creatures filled them with a power we no longer understand.

A demon stands to attention behind the stone. He has a squat, leathery body and a green head, part human, part canine. A large, surly mouth. Four hairy arms and two long legs. Floppy ears. His white eyes are filled with fear, and he holds himself rigidly, as if standing still against his will.

There's a grey window of light a few yards from the stone and demon. In front of it, grinning lopsidedly in her warped, pus- and blood-drenched new form, is the monstrous Juni Swan.

"You took your time getting here," she snarls.

"We stopped for a bite to eat," Dervish quips. Sharmila is studying the demon. Beranabus is looking at Juni with a mixture of sadness and disgust. Kirilli is just gaping.

"What happened to you?" Beranabus asks quietly.

"Don't you like my new body?" Juni croons, posing obscenely. "I preferred my old frame, but this is what I'm stuck with. The price of cheating death."

"How *did* you survive?" Beranabus presses, the pity in his voice vanishing in an instant. "Dervish killed you. I felt your soul leave. Did Lord Loss have the Board with him? Is that how he pulled off this trick?"

Juni shakes her head smugly. "That's for me to know and you to guess, old man." She looks at the rest of us, sneering spitefully. "I told them you'd come. My master said you wouldn't be so foolish, but I knew you would. You're arrogant. You never let the threat of a trap put you off. I always knew your ridiculous self-belief would prove your undoing — and so it has."

Beranabus stares at his ex-assistant, shaken by her hideous appearance and the mad hatred in her expression. "How did it come to this?" he croaks. "Life with me can't have been worse than what you're going through now."

"You don't know what you're talking about," Juni says. "You were far worse than Lord Loss. I serve him willingly, by my own choice, but I was a slave to you, with no say over what happened to me."

"But —" Beranabus starts.

"No!" Juni barks. "You're not worth arguing with." She glares at the rest of us. "You can choose too. You don't have to serve this fool or perish with him. Join me now and live. Stay loyal to him and die."

Dervish laughs. "You've lost your marbles. Nadia Moore would have known that wasn't an option. Even Juni Swan could have seen that it's a no-brainer. But you've become something warped and inhuman. Do you honestly believe any of us would throw in our lot with a thing as twisted and insane as you?"

Juni's lips tremble and the skin around her cheeks cracks in a series of tiny channels. "How dare you speak to me like that!"

"You were my love," Dervish says. "I'll speak to you any way I like."

She starts to curse him, then restrains herself and giggles. "We'll be lovers again, darling Dervish. I'll keep you alive in a body even more wretched than this. I'll lavish you with torment and pain. You'll beg me to kill you, every single day for the rest of time, but I won't."

"Sounds nasty." Dervish yawns.

"Um, I don't know how these things normally work," Kirilli speaks up, "but shouldn't we be ripping her into a million pieces instead of trading insults?"

"Don't knock the insults," Dervish growls. "This is the best part of a fight. If you don't get the digs in at the beginning, there'll be no time later."

"Who is this charlatan?" Juni huffs, glaring at Kirilli.

"A Disciple," Beranabus says. "A friend and assistant, as you once were."

"Assistant only," Juni corrects him. "Never a friend."

"You were Kernel's friend," Sharmila says softly. "You saved his life, even after you had turned traitor. Do you hate him too? Will you kill him along with the rest of us if you get the chance?"

"Without blinking," Juni says coldly. "I warned him not to get in my way again. I might not kill him today — if he has any sense, he'll slip away when the rest of you are dead — but I'll catch up with him soon. It's the end of mankind's reign. Within a year we'll cleanse Earth of its human fungus and take the world forward into a new demonic era. Your precious billions are living on borrowed time, Beranabus, but you reckless fools don't even have that. Which is where Cadaver comes in. . . ." She nods at the demon behind the lodestone.

"Cadaver?" Beranabus frowns.

"He stole the demon that was masquerading as Kernel's brother," Sharmila reminds him.

Cadaver whines and strains his neck. He's not a willing participant in this. He's a prisoner. When he opens his mouth and speaks, we learn who his captor is.

"Greetings, my brave doomed friends."

Cadaver's lips are moving, but the words and accent aren't the demon's — they belong to the sentinel of sorrow, Lord Loss.

"A cheap trick," Beranabus grunts. "Too afraid to face us in person? Reduced to speaking through a puppet?"

"Why not use Cadaver's mouth?" Lord Loss counters, speaking from his realm in the Demonata's universe. "I gave it to him. I could have made use of any of my familiars, but I thought this one most fitting. Such a pity Kernel isn't here. I'm sure Cadaver's appearance would have revived many fond memories."

"I have had enough of this," Sharmila growls. She takes a step forward and raises her hand, taking aim at Cadaver.

"Wait," Beranabus stops her. "He's close to the lodestone. If we kill him, his blood will drench it."

"Will that make a difference?" Sharmila asks.

Beranabus grimaces. "I doubt he's there for show."

"Astute as always," Lord Loss murmurs through the unfortunate Cadaver. "You would have made a fine demon, Beranabus. You have wasted your talent on a far inferior species. But it's not too late to change. Join us. Live forever as one of the rulers of the universes."

"Live forever?" Beranabus laughs. "Nonsense! All things die. That's the nature of existence."

"Nature is about to be reversed," Lord Loss says.

"By whom?" Beranabus asks. "Your shadowy master? What's his name? I can't serve him if I don't even know his name."

Lord Loss tuts. "No names, not unless you join us."

"Well, that's not going to happen," Beranabus sniffs. "And I don't think you really expected me to switch sides. So why are we here? Do you want to gloat before your master kills us?"

"No," Lord Loss says. Cadaver's head swivels and his eyes fix on me. "We want Bec."

Beranabus, Dervish, and Sharmila shuffle towards me, forming a protective barrier. I'm touched by their show of support.

"What do you want with me?" I ask in a small, trembling voice.

"Your piece of the Kah-Gash, of course," Lord Loss says.

Beranabus puts a hand on the nape of my neck. His fingers are shaking. By reading his thoughts, I understand why. Though I'm afraid, I place my hand over his and squeeze, giving my assent.

"You can't have her," Beranabus croaks. "I won't let a piece of the Kah-Gash fall into your foul hands. I'll kill her first."

"But you love her," Lord Loss gasps with mock shock.

"Aye," Beranabus says. "But I'll kill her anyway."

Kirilli is gaping at us, confused and dismayed. Dervish and Sharmila look distraught but resigned.

"Then kill her," Lord Loss purrs, and I catch a glimpse of his wicked leer in Cadaver's terror-stricken eyes. "It makes no difference. If she dies, the piece will be set free and faithful Juni will capture and deliver it to our new master. Death isn't an obstacle to us, not any longer."

Beranabus squints at Cadaver, not sure if this is a bluff.

"The piece was originally mine," Lord Loss says petulantly. "It lay dormant within me for hundreds of thousands of years. But when I shared my magic with Bec, back when I wished to preserve humanity, it slipped from my body into hers." Cadaver shakes a hairy finger at me.

"It can move from one being to another?" Beranabus frowns and his thoughts move quickly. He uses a spell to communicate directly with me. *Give it to me,* he whispers silently. *Pass it on.*

I can't, I reply. *I don't know how.*

"Master," Juni interrupts. "This window will close soon. If I am to return to your side, we must act now."

"Of course," Lord Loss says. "Wait a few moments more, my dear. Then you can come home."

Cadaver bends forward over the lodestone, but his eyes remain rooted on us. "I must say farewell, old friends," Lord Loss murmurs. "I don't think any of you will survive the coming battle. You have caused me much displeasure over the years, but I shall miss you."

His eyes settle on Dervish and he smiles. "Don't worry about how Grubitsch will cope without you. He walked into a trap, just as you did. He will be dead soon if he isn't already."

Dervish hisses and starts to respond, but Lord Loss is looking at Sharmila now. "There will be much chaos before the end," he tells her. "Humanity will be given time to scream before we cleanse the universe of its miserable stain. I will track down those you love and execute them personally. I will lavish extra attention on the children and babies."

Sharmila is close to tears, but she holds them back and curses Lord Loss foully. He chuckles and his gaze flickers to Kirilli. The stage magician braces himself. "Go on," he snarls manfully. "I can take any threat you dish out."

"I don't know who you are and I have no interest in you," Lord Loss says dismissively, and Kirilli deflates.

"Bec," the demon master hums, staring at me directly. "It has been such a long time since our paths —"

"Let's get out of here," I snap, backing away from the lodestone and the mound of dead bodies, having no desire to listen to more of his rhetoric.

"Aye," Beranabus says, retreating beside me. He thrusts a hand in Juni's direction, but she darts through the window before he can strike. A crazy, lingering cackle is her only parting shot at us.

"Very well," Lord Loss sighs. "Let the slaughter commence."

Cadaver's head explodes and the demon's blood soaks the lodestone. It glows beneath the stack of corpses, sucking the blood as it pumps from Cadaver's neck. A bolt of light shoots from the base of the stone, down through the watery layers of the sea, disappearing a second later into the murky depths below.

We should run. It's crazy to linger. But we're held,

captivated, curious to see what will happen. This is new even to Beranabus, who's seen virtually everything in his time.

For a few seconds — nothing. Then a ball of light rises from the darkness of the ocean floor. It's larger than the ball that shot downwards, and expands the closer it comes. There's a dark glob at the center, almost like a pupil in an eye. It's a long way off, but I'm certain it's the Shadow. A strange, tingling energy washes into the ship, saturating the air around us. I've never felt any magic quite like it.

"Enough!" Beranabus shouts. "Let's get out before it tears through the hold and rips us apart."

We surge towards the door, a terrified Kirilli leading the way, Sharmila behind him, then me. Dervish and Beranabus bring up the rear, preparing themselves to fight off the Shadow.

Just before we get to the door, something moves nearby. It's one of the humans. A woman. Her arms are twitching and her head is rising slowly. The demons must have mistakenly left her for dead.

"Wait!" I yell, breaking left. "There's a survivor." I bend over the woman, grab her arms and haul her to her feet. "Come on. We have to get out. I'll help. . . ."

I come to a sickening halt. The woman's face is missing from the nose down. As she gets to her feet, scraps of her brain trickle through the gap where her jaw should be and down her chest. She can't be alive, yet she's looking at me. But not with warmth or gratitude — only with *hunger.*

My mind whirrs and I realize what's happening. But before I can yell a warning, dozens of corpses around us thrash, slither, then rise like dreadful ghouls. *The dead are coming back to life!*

SHIP OF THE LIVING DEAD

✣　　✣　　✣

Bill-E loved zombie films. He thought there was nothing cooler than corpses coming back to life and eating the brains of the living. But I don't think he'd have been thrilled if it happened to him in real life, like it's happening to us now.

The revived dead throw themselves at us slavishly, mindlessly, silently. They move as fluidly as in life, not in the shambling manner of movie zombies. Some are hampered by the loss of limbs and stumble sluggishly. But most are as quick on their feet as any living person.

They look more like living people too. They're not rotting, misshapen monsters. It's easy to rip the head off an inhuman beast from another dimension, but doing that to someone who looks human feels like murder. It's horrible.

The woman I picked off the floor tries to claw my throat open. I shove her away and turn to kick a man in the head before he bites my thigh. Ahead of me, a girl throws herself down the stairs and knocks Kirilli over. She snaps at his left hand and chews off his two smallest fingers. He screams, then sets her aflame, instinct lending him the magical fighting impulse that he previously lacked.

"Zombies!" Dervish snorts with disgust, scattering a handful with a ball of energy. "First werewolves, then demons, now zombies. What will they throw at us next?"

"There might not be a *next*," Sharmila says, helping Kirilli to his feet and shooting a bolt of fire up the stairs. There are shrieks from the zombies above us, and the stench of burning flesh and hair fills the air. Sharmila grimaces, but sends another burst of flames after the first.

"You're not worried about this lot, are you?" Dervish says, sending more of the living corpses flying across the hold. "We can handle them. We've faced a hell of a lot stronger in our time."

"You miss the point," Sharmila replies with forced calm. "The dead are meant only to delay us. There is our true foe." She points to the center of the hold. The ball of light is almost level with the ship. As we watch, it breaks around the hull and disintegrates. A black hissing ball of nightmares explodes through the shield of energy and gathers around the lodestone.

We only got a glimpse of the Shadow that night in the cave. Here, in the lights of the hull, it's revealed in all its furious glory. The creature is the general shape of a giant octopus, about fifty feet broad, thirty feet tall, covered in a mass of countless long writhing tendrils, which whip around the lodestone, tightening and loosening as the creature saps strength from the ancient stone. A few of the living dead wander too close to the lodestone and are beheaded by some of the knifelike tentacles — the Shadow doesn't suffer fools gladly. The beast doesn't seem to have a face, but I'm sure it sees us and is focused upon us.

As I gaze with horror at the massive pulsing creature of shadows, a fat man trailing guts hurls himself at me, gnashing his teeth. I flick him away with the wave of a hand and shuffle closer to Beranabus. He's eyeing the Shadow warily.

"It doesn't feel like a demon," I note.

"I know," he mutters.

"Can we outrun it?"

"We can try."

"The stairs are free," Sharmila calls. "But more of the dead are coming. If we are to flee, we must do so now."

"What are we waiting for?" Kirilli yells. He hasn't managed to cauterise his wound. Blood spurts from the jagged stumps where his fingers used to be.

"You think we can fight it?" Dervish asks, stepping up beside Beranabus.

"I don't know."

The window Juni escaped through blinks out of existence. That seems to decide for Beranabus. "Let's test it," he grunts, moving away from the door, back towards the lodestone. "Maybe it's not as powerful as it thinks."

He unleashes a ball of bright blue magic at the Shadow. The ball strikes the creature directly and crackles around it. Its tendrils thrash wildly, then return to their almost tender caressing of the lodestone. Its body continues to throb. A high piercing sound fills the hold — I think the Shadow's laughing at us.

Sharmila bends, touches the invisible barrier where the floor should be, and creates a pillar of fire. It streaks towards the lodestone, slicing through several zombies on the way. When it reaches the Shadow, Sharmila barks a command and it billows upwards, forming a curtain of flames. The Shadow's consumed, its tendrils retracting like a spider's legs shriveling up. But when the flames die away, it emerges unharmed, oozes over the lodestone, and slides towards us.

Dervish leaps through the air and chops at a thick tendril. He cuts clean through it, severing the tip. The amputated piece dissolves before it hits the floor, crumbling away to ash.

The Shadow catches Dervish with another tentacle, roughly shakes him, then flings him across the hold. Beranabus halts Dervish's flight, and the spiky-haired mage drops to the floor a few feet in front of the magician, gasping with pain, his skin burnt a bright pink where the tendril touched him.

"Stuff this!" Kirilli pants, and darts up the stairs. I let him run. No point trying to make him fight if he doesn't want to. Besides, I doubt he could make much of a difference.

About a dozen walking corpses converge on me. I work a quick blinding spell, then plow through them as they mill around. I squat by Dervish as Beranabus and Sharmila engage the Shadow, and swiftly cool his burnt flesh.

"Are you OK?" I ask as he sits up, dazed.

"Three," he mutters. When I frown, he smiles sheepishly. "Sorry. I thought you asked how many fingers you were holding up."

I help him to his feet. He gulps when he looks at the Shadow, but advances to try again.

"What can I do?" I shout at Beranabus.

"Get out," he roars. "You're the one it's after."

"But I can't —"

"Go!"

Cursing, I turn and run. Before I'm even halfway to the door, I feel a whoosh of hot air on my back. Glancing over my shoulder, I see the Shadow directly behind me. It's swept past Beranabus and his Disciples, barreling them aside. They lie sprawled on the invisible floor. They're picking themselves up, turning to help me — but too late.

The Shadow seizes me with several tentacles and lifts me high into the air. I scream, pain filling all parts of my body at once. It's like being on fire, except the agony cuts deeper than any natural flame, burning through flesh and bone, turning my blood to vapor.

I somehow hold myself together. It takes every last bit of magic that I possess, but I fight the terrible, fiery clutch of the Shadow and wildly restore blood, bones and flesh as it grips me tighter and tries to fry me again. I'm absorbing memories from the beast, mostly garbled, but what I comprehend is more terrifying than I would have considered possible.

The Shadow's surprised I'm still alive. It meant to slaughter me and absorb the freed piece of the Kah-Gash. But it's not dismayed by my resistance. The beast is much stronger than me and knows it simply has to keep applying pressure. I can last a matter of seconds, no more. Then . . .

Beranabus is suddenly beside me, bellowing like a madman. He slashes at the tentacles, slicing through them as easily as Dervish did. The Shadow is more of a menace than any demon I've ever faced, but it's insubstantial. It's not by nature a physical creature. It can easily and quickly replace what we destroy, but it can't harden itself against our blows.

I fall free, and Beranabus drags me away. Sharmila and Dervish dart into the gap we've left and attack the Shadow with bolts of energy and fire. It makes a squealing noise and lashes at them with its tentacles. They duck and dodge the blows, punching and kicking at the tendrils.

"Go!" Beranabus gasps, and tries to throw me ahead of him.

"Wait," I cry, holding on. "I know what it is."

"Tell me later," he roars. "There's no time now."

He's right. I won't have the chance to explain, not with words. But I have to let him know. He thinks he can defeat this beast, that if they keep working on the tendrils, they'll eventually chop their way through to the body. He believes they can kill it, like any other demon.

He's wrong.

I clutch his small clean hands and use the same spell he used earlier to bypass the need for words. He gasps as I force-feed him the information. Then his eyes widen and a look of shocked desperation crosses his face.

"*How?*" he croaks.

"I don't know," I sob.

Sharmila screams. The Shadow has ripped one of her legs loose. It rains to the floor in a shower of bones and flesh. A few of the zombies fall on the remains with vicious delight.

Beranabus is thinking hard and fast, trying to turn this in our favor. He's always been able to outwit demons who were certain they'd gotten the better of him. Even in recent years, ancient, battered, befuddled, his cunning gave him a crucial advantage. He can't believe it will fail him now, but he's never had to deal with anything like the Shadow.

The lines of his face go smooth. He half-nods, and his lips twitch at the corners. My heart leaps with hope. He's seen something. He has a plan!

"Tell Kernel," he wheezes, standing straight and scattering a horde of zombies as if swatting flies. "Tell him to find me."

"You want me to send Kernel down?" I frown. "But he's not a fighter. He —"

"Just tell him to find me," Beranabus sighs, then bends and kisses my forehead. "I loved you as a child, Bec, and I love you still. I always will."

Through the brief contact, I catch a glimpse of what he's planning. It's perilous. He probably won't make it out alive. But it's the only way. Our only hope.

"Don't watch," he says, and his voice is guttural, unnatural, as his vocal cords begin to thicken and change. "I don't want you to see me like this."

He whirls away and bellows at the Shadow, an inhuman challenge. Dervish and Sharmila glance back, astonished by the ferocity of the roar. Their faces crumple when they see what Beranabus is becoming.

I back away slowly, but I can't obey Beranabus's final command. I have to look. Besides, he thought my feelings would alter if I saw him in his other form, but they won't. If you truly love someone, you don't care what they look like.

Beranabus is transforming. He outgrows his suit, which falls away from him like a banana peel. His skin splits and unravels. Bones snap out of his head, then lengthen, fresh flesh forming around them. Muscles bulge on his arms and legs like pustulant sores. They burst, then reform, even larger than before. Tough, dark skin replaces his natural covering. Only it's not really skin — more like scales.

A tail forces its way out through the small of Beranabus's back. It grows to six feet . . . ten . . . fifteen. Spikes poke out of it, as well as several mouths full of sharp teeth and forked tongues.

I catch sight of his face. Purplish, scaly skin. Dark grey eyes, round like a fly's, utterly demonic. His mouth is three times the size of my head, filled with fangs that look more like stalactites and stalagmites than teeth. Yellowish blood streams from his nose, but he takes no notice. Raising his massive arms, he pushes through the undulating nest of tentacles and hammers a fist at the Shadow, driving it back.

"What the hell is that?" Dervish croaks, backing up beside me, helping the one-legged Sharmila along.

"Beranabus," I answer quietly. "The Bran we never saw. The demon side that he kept shackled. This is what he would have looked like if he'd let his father's genes run free, if he'd chosen the way of the Demonata."

Beranabus lashes the Shadow with his tail. The spikes rip through the shadowy wisps of its body, the teeth snapping at it, tearing open holes. The Shadow shrieks angrily but the holes quickly close and the beast fights without pause, smothering Beranabus with its tentacles.

Dervish, Sharmila, and I are by the doorway. We should take advantage of the situation and race up the stairs. But we're mesmerized. We can't flee without knowing the outcome. Sharmila clears the stairs of zombies to keep the route out of the hold open, but she doesn't take her eyes off the battling pair.

"Can he control himself like that?" she asks quietly as the behemoths wrestle.

"Not for long," I whisper. "This is the first time he's completely unchained his beastly half. If he maintains that shape and lets the monster run free too long, it will take over."

"How much time does he have?" Dervish asks.

"He doesn't know. He's not even sure he *can* turn back again. Maybe he's given it too much freedom. The Beranabus we knew could be gone forever. He might turn against us and work with the Shadow to destroy mankind."

Dervish and Sharmila stare at me as if I'm the one who's changed shape.

"Why would he take such a risk?" Sharmila gasps.

"He had to. I'll explain later. If we survive."

The beast that was Beranabus shrugs free of the Shadow's tentacles and staggers away. For an awful moment I think that he's about to attack us. But then he bellows at the Shadow and darts past it, making for the lodestone.

"Ah!" Sharmila exclaims with sudden hope. "If he breaks the stone . . ."

". . . the Shadow will be sucked back to its own universe," I finish.

"We hope," Dervish adds gloomily.

Finding its path to me unexpectedly clear, the Shadow lunges forward, eager to finish me off. Then it pauses. It doesn't glance back — as I noted earlier, it doesn't have a face — but it's somehow analyzing Beranabus. There's a brief moment of consideration — can it kill me and steal the power of the Kah-Gash before Beranabus breaks the stone?

The Shadow decides the odds are against it and reverses direction, launching itself at the transformed magician. It catches him just before he reaches the lodestone. The pair spin past. Beranabus roars with frustration as he shoots beyond his target. The Shadow whips him with its tentacles. Deep cuts open across his arms and legs, and many of the protective scales on his chest and back shatter under the force of the blows.

Just before they fly out of striking distance of the lodestone, Beranabus's tail twitches. The tip catches a notch in the stone and Beranabus jerks to a halt. The Shadow loses its grip and ends up in a heap. It's back on its tentacles within seconds, but Beranabus has already jerked himself within reach of the lodestone.

He grabs the stone with his massive hands and exerts great pressure, trying to snap it in half. There's a cracking sound, and a split forms in the uppermost tip of the rock. But then it holds and although Beranabus strains harder, it doesn't divide any further.

The Shadow hurls itself at Beranabus and lands on his back. Tendrils jab at him from all directions, destroying his scaly armor, penetrating the flesh beneath. One of his grey eyes pops. Several of his fangs are ripped from his jaw. Blood flies from him in jets and fountains.

Beranabus howls with agony, but otherwise ignores the assault and focuses on the lodestone. He's still trying to tear it in two. The stone is pulsing. The split at the top increases a few inches. The gap's just wide enough for Beranabus to jam his unnaturally large fingers into it. Snapping at the Shadow with the remains of his fangs, he transfers his grip to the crack, gets the tips of all his fingers inside, and tugs.

There's a creaking sound, then a snapping noise, and the stone splits down the middle to about a third of the way from the top. Beranabus yells with triumph, wraps both arms around the severed chunk of rock and rips it free of the lodestone, tossing it to the floor like an oversized ball of waste.

The Shadow screeches and scuttles after the rock, perhaps hoping to reattach it. I quickly unleash my power and send the piece of stone shooting across the hold. It smashes into the side of the ship and explodes in a cascade of pebbly splinters.

Beranabus roars with ghastly, demonic laughter and bites into one of the Shadow's tentacles. As he rips it off, another tendril strikes the side of his head and slices through to his brain. The triumph that had blossomed within me vanishes instantly.

"Bran!" I scream, and dart towards him. Dervish holds me back.

The Shadow strikes repeatedly at Beranabus in a tempestuous rage. It gouges great chunks of flesh from his chest and stomach. Scraps of lung, slivers of a heart and other internal organs splatter the broken lodestone. Then, in a childish sulk, the Shadow tosses him aside like an old doll it's finished playing with.

The demonic beast that Beranabus has become rolls over several times before coming to a rest near the side of the hull. Again I try to race to his aid, but Dervish has a firm hold and doesn't let go even when I bite him.

Beranabus raises his huge, transformed, scaly head. He glances at the Shadow and the lodestone with his one bulbous grey eye and grins. Then his head swivels and he looks for me. When he finds me struggling with Dervish, his grin softens, and I see a trace of the Beranabus I knew in the expression. I also see the boy he once was — scatterbrained Bran. He smiles at me foolishly, the way Bran used to, and gurgles something. I think he's trying to say *"Flower."*

Then the grey light in his eye dims and extinguishes. The smile turns into a tired sneer. He coughs up yellow blood and tries to drag himself forward. But the strength drains from his arms. His body sags. A jagged breath dances from his lips, and his head drops. By the time his forehead connects with the cold steel floor of the hold, the three-thousand-year-old legend is part of this world no more.

GOING DOWN

✠   ✠   ✠

In desperation the Shadow clambers after me, but a funnel has formed in the water beneath the broken lodestone. It stretches far down and whirls violently, creating a magical vacuum that drags at the mass of shadows. The beast's rear tentacles are stiff behind it, drawn towards the vortex, and its body begins to lengthen and narrow. The creature strains against it, but the vacuum is too strong. There are laws that even the Shadow has to obey, at least for the time being.

In a rush, and with a hateful shriek, the Shadow's ripped away. It smashes through the lodestone, shattering the remains of the rock, and disappears down the funnel, howling all the way. Moments later the funnel collapses in on itself as swiftly as it formed.

I want to rush to Beranabus's corpse and bid him farewell. I'm weeping, and all I want is to be by my dead friend's side. But that's not possible. Because now that the lodestone's magic has evaporated, the shield keeping the sea at bay has started to give way.

The fragments of the lodestone fall first, trickling through cracks in the invisible barrier. Water seeps up through the cracks, spreading neatly across the surface of the shield. Then one of the living dead stumbles and drops out of sight, as if crashing through a thin layer of ice.

"Let's get the hell out of here!" Dervish shouts, hauling me through the door.

"Beranabus!" I cry.

"We can't help him now," Dervish pants. As he says it, the shield flickers out of existence and water floods the hold.

The ship lurches. A wave of foaming water surges towards us, washing away the helpless bodies of the zombies. We should be washed away too, but Sharmila acts swiftly to avert catastrophe, establishing a barrier around us and the doorway. The wave breaks and seethes away, the sea temporarily cheated of its victims.

"Quick," Sharmila gasps, hopping up the stairs. "The magic is fading. The barrier will not hold."

She's right. I can feel the energy ebbing away at a frightening rate. I look one last time for the body of Beranabus, but the ocean has already claimed it. Wiping tears from my cheeks, I hurry after Dervish and Sharmila, knowing that if we don't climb sharply, we'll soon be joining Beranabus in his watery grave.

✠ We move a lot slower going up than we did coming down. It's not just the fact that we're climbing. We're tired and drained. We were fine when the air was thick with magic, but the unnatural energy is fading fast.

We're halfway up the second flight of stairs when I hear

the sea gush up the corridors behind us. I've no idea how long we have. I imagine it would usually take a ship this size at least a couple of hours to sink, but the hole in the hull was extremely large.

The zombies are still going strong. The strange magic of the Shadow that reanimated them is fading slower than the energy we were tapping into. While we're rapidly weakening, the zombies haven't been significantly affected.

We don't use bolts of magic anymore or arrogantly dismiss them with a wave of a hand. We're reduced to close-quarters fighting. We can still repel them with our charged fists and feet — the magic hasn't disappeared entirely — but there are thousands of zombies. If we're still here when the last of the energy fades, they'll swamp us. Unless the sea claims us first.

Sharmila's second leg fragments. She pumps magic into it to hold the bones and scraps of flesh together.

"Don't bother," Dervish grunts, lifting her. "Save your energy. Get on my back. I'll be your legs. You keep the zombies off."

"What about your heart?" Sharmila shouts.

"It'll hold for a while."

I can move much quicker than Dervish now that he's burdened with Sharmila. I'm tempted to race ahead of them, up through the ship, away from the encroaching water. But they're my friends, and they wouldn't desert me if I was in their position. If it becomes necessary to flee, I will. But as long as there's a chance we might all make it out alive, I'll stick with them.

I take the lead, knocking flailing, snarling zombies out of our way, pushing ahead, the undead humans crowding the staircase behind and in front. I should feel fear in the face of such warped, nightmarish foes, but my emotions are focused on Beranabus — there's only room within me for mourning.

I can't believe he's dead. It's hard to imagine a world without the ancient magician. He's been mankind's savior for longer than anyone should have to serve. What will we do without him? I doubt the Disciples can repel the waves of Demonata attacks by themselves. Beranabus believed our universe created heroes in times of need. If that's true, perhaps someone will replace him. But it's hard to picture anybody taking the magician's place. He was one of a kind.

We hit another level. I'm about to lurch up the next set of stairs when I spot Kirilli Kovacs tussling with a gaggle of zombies. He's in bad shape, bitten and scratched all over. A dozen of the living dead surround him.

I should leave him. He doesn't really deserve to be rescued, and I can't afford to waste any of my dwindling power. But I can't turn my back on a man just because he's a coward. Kirilli didn't betray or undermine us — he simply gave in to fear, as many people would have.

Drawing on my reserves, I mutter a spell and gesture at the zombies packed around Kirilli. They fly apart, and a path opens. "Run!" I yell. Kirilli doesn't need to be told twice. He stumbles clear of the zombies and is by my side moments later. Blood cakes his face, but his eyes are alert behind the red veil. He starts to say something.

"No time for talking," I snap. "Get up those stairs quick, and if you fall, I'll leave you."

Kirilli flinches, draws a breath, then darts ahead of me, taking pole position, staggering up the seemingly endless flights of steps towards the upper deck and its promise of escape.

✠ As we're forcing our way up another staircase clogged with zombies, Dervish gasps and collapses to his knees. One hand darts to his chest. I think it's the end of him, but Sharmila presses her hands over his and channels magic into his heart. She pulls a stricken face as she helps — the magic she's directing into his flesh means she has less to ward off the pain in her legs. But she has no real choice. Without Dervish to carry her, she's doomed.

Kirilli is struggling with the zombies. He's weak and afraid. He lashes out at them wildly, not preserving his energy or channeling it wisely. I've tried warning him, but he either doesn't hear me or can't respond. He knows only one thing — he has to go up. That's tattooed on his brain, driving him on.

Thankfully the walking corpses are moving more like regular zombies now. Their magic is fading. The attacks are clumsier, less coordinated. But they're still on their feet, our scent thick in their nostrils, licking their lips at the thought of biting into our soft, juicy brains.

✠ As we hit the last step of another flight, Kirilli screams something unintelligible. I'm exhausted, but I push forward in reply to his cry, fearing the worst. But when I clear the step, I realize it was a yell of exhilaration, not dismay. We're back at the upper deck.

The ship is lurching at a worrysome angle, and the deck is littered with hordes of zombies. But we get a fresh burst of hope when we breathe the fresh, salty air.

Dervish lays Sharmila down and squats beside her. "I need . . . a minute," he wheezes, face ashen, rubbing his chest.

"We can't stop," Kirilli shrieks, knocking over a zombie in uniform who's either the ship's captain or a highly placed mate.

"Shut up," I growl, and crouch next to Dervish. "Let me help."

"No," he mutters. "Save your magic . . . for yourself."

"Don't be a fool." I shove his hands away and rest my left palm on his chest. I pump magic into him, enough to keep him from keeling over.

"Do you know the way back to Kernel?" Sharmila asks, wincing from the pain in her thighs. They're bleeding at the stumps, the flesh we knotted together in the demon universe coming undone.

"Yes." I grin at her. "Perfect memory, remember?"

She returns the smile, but shakily. "Perhaps you should leave me here."

"We're not leaving anyone behind," I say firmly. "Except maybe Kirilli."

He stares at me with a wounded expression. "I hope you don't —" he starts.

"Not now," I stop him. My cheeks are dry. I must have stopped weeping at some point coming up the stairs. The ship is slipping farther into the water. The angle of the deck to the sea is increasing steadily. Kernel's at the end of the ship that is rising. If we don't act quickly, we won't make it.

"Come on," I command. "One last push. We can rest once we slip through the window."

Dervish sighs wearily but staggers to his feet. He reaches for Sharmila. "Wait," I tell him, and glance fiercely at Kirilli. "It's time you proved yourself worthy of rescue. Carry her."

"But I have a bad back," he protests. "I never lift anything heavier than —"

"Carry her," I repeat myself, "or I'll cut your legs off, glue them to Sharmila, and let her walk out of here on *your* feet."

Kirilli gives a little cry of horror. He suspects I'm bluffing, but he's uncertain.

"I am not that heavy," Sharmila chuckles. "Especially without my legs."

"We're nearly there," I tell the stage magician. "You won't have to carry her far."

"Very well," Kirilli snaps. "But if I throw my back out of joint, I'll sue." He flashes me a feeble grin and picks up Sharmila. I help settle her on his back, then push through the zombies converging on us, lashing out with both my small fists, praying for the strength to stay on my feet long enough to guide us all to safety.

✠ I'm almost fully drained. Only a sheer stubborn streak keeps me going. I refuse to fall this close to the end. It happened before, in the cave all those centuries ago. I almost made it out. I could see the exit as the rock ground shut around it. It was horrible to come up short with freedom in sight. I won't taste that defeat again.

Deck chairs and unbolted fixtures slide down the deck. Some of the zombies topple and slide too. Extra obstacles for us to dodge. The end of the ship continues to rise out of the water. A few more minutes and the angle will be too steep to climb. We'll slip backwards to perish with the zombies when the ship's dragged under.

We catch sight of the swimming pool. The window's still open, and Kernel's in front of it. But he's struggling with a zombie. There are dozens around him and the window, separated from them by a circle of magic. But one has pierced his defenses and is wrestling with him.

"Kernel!" I cry. "Hold on. We're almost with you. We —"

Kernel shouts something in response. He tries to tear himself away from the zombie, then reaches for its head to rip it loose — it's only attached by jagged strips of flesh to the neck. There's a flash of blinding light and we all cover our eyes, Kirilli dropping Sharmila out of necessity.

When I open my eyes a few seconds later, it's like looking at a bright light through several layers of plastic. I blink furiously to clear my vision. When I can see properly, I look for Kernel. The circle where he was is still in place. The zombies around it are all momentarily sightless, stumbling into each other, rubbing their eyes.

But the window is gone. And where it stood — where Kernel and the zombie were battling — is an ugly swill of tattered flesh, clumps of guts, fragments of bones, and several pints of wasted human blood.

THE ONLY WAY

✠　　✠　　✠

STUNNED, I stare at the spot where Kernel and the window were. I'm not sure what happened. Where did the explosion of light come from? Are those the remains of Kernel and the zombie, or just one of them? Did Kernel slip through the window before it closed or did he perish here, the window blinking out of existence along with its creator?

"Is he dead?" Dervish roars, smashing the nose of a zombie that was about to sink its teeth into my skull.

"I don't know."

"Sharmila?"

She shakes her head uncertainly.

Dervish doesn't bother to ask Kirilli. He glances around, desperation lending a wild look to his already strained features. "The lifeboats," he mutters. "We have to get away from here or we'll be sucked under."

"But —" I begin.

"No time," he barks, staggering towards the nearest lifeboat. "Come on. Don't stand there gaping."

Kirilli moans and stumbles after Dervish, picking up Sharmila without having to be told. She punches weakly at a couple of zombies, not much strength left. We're all firing on our final cylinders. Only the promise of escape keeps us going. But I've thought of something Dervish hasn't. Escape will be more complicated than he thinks.

✠ Dervish is working on a lifeboat when I reach him. He doesn't have the magic to release it, so he's having to manually lower it over the side. Kirilli is helping.

"We had a safety drill a few days ago," Kirilli boasts. "Leave it to me. I know what to do. If we pull this lever here . . ."

"That's where the oar goes," Dervish growls, pushing Kirilli aside.

The lifeboat slides towards the edge of the ship but comes to a sudden halt just above the rails. "It's stuck," Dervish grunts, pushing at it, looking for something — anything — else to pull.

"No," I sigh, keeping an eye on several zombies heading our way. "It's the barrier. The ship's still encased in a bubble of magic."

"Nonsense," Dervish snorts. "That's gone. My heart wouldn't be hammering like a pneumatic drill if —"

"The barrier's still there," I stop him. "I don't know how, but it is." I point at the nearest zombie, a woman a long way ahead of the others. "Kirilli, grab her and throw her overboard."

"With pleasure," Kirilli says — the zombie is much smaller than he is. He runs across, picks her up, and chucks her over the rail. She bounces off an invisible wall and lands on top of Kirilli. As she chews his left forearm he squeals and wriggles free. He kicks her hard, then glares at me. "You knew that was going to happen!"

I ignore the irate conjuror and lock gazes with Dervish. The fight has sapped his strength. He looks like an old man ready for death.

"The barrier might crumble before the ship sinks," Sharmila suggests, more out of wretched hope than any real conviction.

"It's as strong as when we arrived," I disagree. "We could have maybe swum out through the hole in the bottom — the barrier must be breached there, since the water's coming in — but we can't get back to the hold to try."

"The zombies!" Dervish cries, coming alive again. "We can use them to punch a hole through the barrier. I did that in Slawter, exploded a demon against the wall of energy. It worked there — it can work here."

"I'm not sure," I mutter, but Dervish has already set his sights on a zombie. Finding extra power from somewhere, he sends the dead person flying against the invisible barrier and holds it there with magic.

"Sharmila," he grunts. "Blast it!"

The old Indian lady tries to focus, but she's too exhausted.

"Leave this to me," Kirilli says, preening himself like an action movie hero. He slides a playing card out from underneath his torn, chewed sleeve, takes careful aim and fires it at the zombie. When it strikes he shouts, "Abracadabra!" and the card and zombie explode.

"There," Kirilli smirks. "I'm not as useless as you thought, am I?"

"Nobody could be," Dervish murmurs, but the humor is forced. The explosion hasn't dented the barrier. It holds as firmly as before.

"They're not powerful enough," I note sadly, felling another zombie as it attacks. "The magic they're working off of isn't the same as ours. They're puppets of the Shadow, not real creatures of magic. We could butcher a thousand against the barrier, but it won't work any better than exploding normal humans."

"That's why Juni sent the demons back to their own universe," Dervish groans. "So we couldn't use them if we got away from the Shadow."

"Lord Loss isn't a fool." I smile sadly. "He learns from his mistakes."

"We're finished," Dervish says miserably.

"Aye," I sigh, unconsciously mimicking Beranabus. "All that's left to determine is whether the zombies eat us or if we drown in the deep blue sea."

I stare at the ranks of living dead shuffling towards us. The Shadow's magic is dwindling. Many of the zombies have fallen and lie twitching or still, returned to the lifeless state from which the Shadow roused them. But a lot remain active, clambering up from the lower levels, massing and advancing, hunched over against the sharp, angled incline of the deck. If the ship doesn't sink within the next few minutes, they'll overwhelm us.

"I don't want to drown," Kirilli says softly. "I've always been afraid of that. I'd rather be eaten." He tugs at the tattered threads of his jacket, trying to make himself presentable. Facing the oncoming hordes, he takes a deep breath and starts towards them.

"Wait," Sharmila stops him. She's smiling faintly. "Disciples never quit. Zahava must have taught you that. We carry on even when all seems lost. When dealing with matters magical, there is always hope."

"She's right," I tell him. "If Kernel's alive, he might open another window and rescue us. Or I could be wrong about the barrier. Maybe it will vanish before the ship sinks and we can clamber overboard."

"What are the odds?" Kirilli asks.

"Slim," I admit. "But you don't want to surrender to the zombies, only to spot the rest of us slipping free at the last second, do you?"

Kirilli squints at me, struggling to decide.

"Actually I was not planning on a miracle," Sharmila says. "We have the power to save ourselves. We do not need to rely on divine intervention."

"What are you talking about?" Dervish frowns.

"There is a way out," Sharmila says. "We can blow a hole in the barrier."

"You've sensed a demon?" I cry, doing a quick sweep of the ship, but finding nothing except ourselves and the zombies.

"No," Sharmila says. "We do not need demons." She looks peaceful, much younger than her years. "*We* are beings of magic."

Dervish's expression goes flat. So does mine. We understand what she's saying. As one, our heads turn, and we stare at Kirilli.

"What?" he growls suspiciously.

"No," Sharmila chuckles. "I was not thinking of poor Kirilli. I doubt he would volunteer and we are not, I hope, prepared to turn on one of our own and murder him like a pack of savages."

"We'll draw lots," Dervish says quickly. "Kirilli too, whether he likes it or not."

"Draw lots for *what*?" Kirilli shouts, still clueless.

"There will be no lottery," Sharmila says firmly. "Bec is too young and Kirilli is not willing."

"Fine," Dervish huffs. "That leaves me and you. Fifty-fifty."

"No," Sharmila says. "You must be a father to Bec. She has lost Beranabus. She cannot afford to lose you too."

"Wait a minute . . . " Dervish huffs.

"Please," Sharmila sighs. "I have no legs. I am the oldest. I have no dependants. And I am now too weak to be of any use — I do not think I could find the power to kill you even if you talked me into letting you take my place."

Dervish gulps and looks to me for help. He wants to persuade her not to do this, to let him be the one who goes out in a blaze of glory.

"Everything she says makes sense," I mumble, practical as always.

"Quickly," Sharmila snaps. "There is almost no magic left. It might be too late already. If you do not act now, it will fade entirely and we will all be lost."

"You're a stubborn old cow, aren't you?" Dervish scowls.

"When I have to be." She smiles.

Dervish checks with me, and I nod sadly. We move side

by side and link hands. Focusing, we unite our meager scraps of magic. I wave a hand at Sharmila, and she slides across the deck, coming to a stop next to the invisible barrier. She sits up and wipes blood from her cheeks. She smiles at us one last time, then serenely closes her eyes and places her hands together. Her lips move softly in prayer.

Dervish howls, partly to direct our magic, partly out of horror. I howl too. Blue light flashes from our fingertips and strikes Sharmila in the chest. The light drills into her head, snapping it back. For a moment her form holds and I fear our power won't be strong enough.

Then the light crackles and a split second later Sharmila explodes. Her bones, guts, flesh and blood splatter the barrier behind her, while the unleashed energy hammers through the shield, creating a porthole to freedom.

We're both shaken and crying, but we have to act swiftly or Sharmila will have died for nothing. We try nudging the lifeboat over to the hole in the barrier but the restraints won't let it be moved in that direction. Weary beyond belief, I yell for Kirilli to join us. When we link hands, I draw on his energy — he hasn't used as much as we have, so he has a fair supply in reserve. I snap the ropes and chains holding the lifeboat in place. Guided by us, it glides through the air, inches above the deck. We shuffle along after it.

When the boat is level with the gap, I edge forward, dragging the others with me, refusing to focus on the gory remains of Sharmila that decorate the rim of the hole. I glance over the rails. We're high up in the air. The water's a long way down. Two options. We can let the boat drop and try to scale down to it. Or . . .

"Climb in," I grunt.

"Will it fit?" Kirilli asks, studying the lifeboat, then the hole, trying to make accurate measurements of both. Typical man!

"Just get in, you fool!" I shout. "That hole could snap shut in a second."

Kirilli scrambles in. When the contact breaks, the lifeboat drops and lands on the deck with a clang. I push Dervish ahead of me, then crawl in after him. The zombies are almost upon us, mewling with hunger.

I grab Kirilli's left hand and Dervish's right. Focusing the last vestiges of our pooled magic, I yell at the lifeboat and send it shooting ahead.

It catches in the hole, jolts forward a few inches under pressure from me, then stalls. It's too wide. We're stuck. Worse — it's plugged the hole, so we can't try jumping to safety. What a useless, stupid way to —

The lifeboat pops free with a sharp, creaking noise. We shoot clear of the hole, the barrier, and the ship, gathering momentum. We sail through the air like some kind of crazily designed bird. We're whooping and cheering.

Then, before any of us realizes the danger of our situation, we hit the sea hard. The boat flips over. I bang my head on the side. My mouth fills as I spill into the sea. I try to spit the water out, but I haven't the energy. As I sink slowly, I raise my eyes and steal one last look at the sky through the liquid layers above me. Then the world turns black.

ALL AT SEA

✠   ✠   ✠

ARMS squeeze my stomach and I vomit. My eyes flutter open and I groan. My head's hanging over the edge of the lifeboat, bits of my last meal bobbing up and down in the water beneath me. I know from the memories flooding into me that Dervish is doing the squeezing.

"It's OK," I groan as he tenses his arms to try again. "I'm alive."

Dervish gently tugs me back over the side. There's water in the bottom. Kirilli is bailing it out with his hands. But we're afloat, and the lifeboat doesn't look like it sustained any major damage.

"We thought we'd lost you," Dervish says, smiling with relief. "Kirilli fished you out, but you were motionless. . . ." He clears his throat and brushes wet hair back from my eyes. The tenderness in his expression warms me more than the sun.

"Have I been unconscious long?" I ask.

"No."

"The ship . . . ?"

"Still there."

Dervish helps me sit up, and we gaze at the sinking vessel. It's listing sharply. It can't last much longer. We're quite far away from it, but if I squint I can make out the shapes of zombies throwing themselves through the hole in pursuit of us. They don't last long once they hit the water.

Kirilli stops bailing and studies the ship with us. We don't say a word. It's a weird sensation, watching something so huge and majestic sink out of sight. It's as if the ship is a living creature that's dying. I feel strangely sad for it.

"All those people," Dervish sighs as the last section slips beneath the waves in a froth of angry bubbles. "I wish we could have saved them."

"Beranabus," I whisper, fresh tears welling in my eyes. "Sharmila. Kernel."

"A costly day's work," Dervish says bitterly. "And we didn't even destroy the Shadow. It'll come after us again. We've lost our leader and two of the strongest Disciples. If Lord Loss was telling the truth, Grubbs is probably dead too. Hardly counts as a victory, does it?"

He doesn't know how true that is. I start to tell him what I learned about the Shadow, but Kirilli interrupts.

"When I left you in the hold," he says shiftily, "I hope you didn't think I was running off. I just wanted to make sure the stairs and corridors were clear, so we could make a quick getaway together."

"Of course," Dervish murmurs. "It never crossed our thoughts that you might have lost your nerve and fled like a cowardly rat, leaving the rest of us in the lurch. You're a hero, Kirilli."

Dervish claps sarcastically, and Kirilli looks aside miserably. I put my hands over Dervish's and stop him. "Don't," I croak. "He helped us in the end. We couldn't have escaped without him."

"I suppose," Dervish mutters.

Kirilli looks up hopefully. "You mean that?"

"We'd never have shifted this boat ourselves," I assure him. "We needed your magic. If you'd fought in the hold and used up your power, we'd have all died."

"Then it worked out for the best." Kirilli beams. "I did the right thing running. I thought so. When I was down there, sizing up the situation, I —"

"Don't push your luck," Dervish growls. Then he narrows his eyes and studies Kirilli closely. "Are those bite marks?"

"Yes," Kirilli says pitifully. He stares at the stumps where his fingers were bitten off. He must have unwittingly used magic to stop the bleeding, scab over the flesh and numb the pain. He'll be screeching like a banshee once the spell fades.

"Those beasts bit and clawed me all over," Kirilli says sulkily, ripping a strip off a sleeve to wrap around the stumps. "I'm lucky they didn't puncture any vital veins or arteries. If I hadn't fought so valiantly, they'd have eaten me alive."

"Such a shame," Dervish purrs, shaking his head.

"What?" Kirilli frowns.

"You've seen a few zombie films in your time, haven't you?"

"One or two," Kirilli sniffs. "I don't like horror films. Why?"

"You must know, then, that their saliva is infectious. When

a zombie bites one of the living, that person succumbs to the disease and turns —"

"No!" Kirilli cries, dropping the strip of shirt and lurching to his feet. "You're joking! You must be!"

Dervish shrugs. "I'm only telling you what I've seen in the movies. It might all be nonsense, but when you think about it logically . . ."

As Kirilli's face crumples, Dervish winks at me. I stifle a smile. This isn't nice, but Kirilli deserves it. Not for being a coward, but for trying to lie. A good scare will do him no harm at all.

✠ We drift for hours. The sun descends. Night claims the sky. After letting Kirilli fret for an hour, Dervish finally told him it was a joke. Kirilli cursed us foully and imaginatively. But he calmed down after a while, and we've been silent since, bobbing about, absorbing the refreshing rays of the sun, thinking about the dead.

It all seems hopeless without Beranabus, especially knowing what I do about the Shadow. Mankind has reached breaking point, and I can't see any way forward. I doubt if even Beranabus could have made a difference. There are some things you can't fight. Certain outcomes are inevitable.

Kirilli has spent the last few minutes examining the lifeboat, scouring it from bow to stern. He returns to his seat with a bottle of water and a small medical box. "Good news and bad," he says, opening the box and looking for ointment to use on his wounds. The healing spell must have passed because he's grimacing. "The good news — both oars are on-board, and there are six bottles of water and this medical box. The bad news — there's no radio equipment or food, and once we drink the water we can't replace it."

"Do you know if the crew of the ship sent a distress signal?" Dervish asks.

"No idea. Even if they did, would it have penetrated the magical barrier?"

"Probably not," Dervish sighs. "Can I have some water?"

Kirilli takes a swig, then passes it across. "Not too much," he warns. "That has to last."

Dervish chuckles drily. "It'll probably last longer than me. My heart could pop any minute."

"Let me check." I place my hand on his chest and concentrate. I can sense the erratic beat of his heart. He's in very poor condition. He needs hospitalization or magic. If we could cross to the universe of the Demonata, we'd be fine.

I try absorbing power from the air, to open a window, but there's virtually nothing to tap into, and I'm in a sorry state. The moon will lend me strength when it rises, but it won't be enough.

"Were you trying to open a window?" Dervish asks softly.

"Yes."

"No joy?"

"I'll be able to later, when I'm stronger," I lie. But Dervish sees through me.

"No tears," he croaks as I start to cry. "Don't waste the moisture."

"It's OK," Kirilli says, trying to cheer me up. "Even if there was no distress signal, the ship's absence will be noted. The seas are monitored by computers and satellites. Most passengers had cell phones and were in regular contact with family and work colleagues. They'll be missed. I bet there'll be an army of planes, helicopters and ships out here by dawn."

"What if we've drifted so far they can't find us?" Dervish asks.

"We can do without the pessimism, thank you," Kirilli protests.

Dervish laughs, then his expression mellows. "Listen," he says earnestly, "if I do croak and help doesn't come, I want you to use my remains. Understand?"

"I'm not sure I do." I frown.

"There's not much meat on these bones, but it'll keep you going for —"

"No!" I shout. "Don't be obscene."

"I'm being practical," he says. "I'm letting you know I won't object if —"

"There'll be no cannibalism on this boat," I growl. "Right, Kirilli?"

"He has a point," Kirilli mutters. "He wouldn't just be a food source — humans are seventy percent water. And we could use his skin for shelter. His bones might come in handy too, if we have to fight off sharks or —"

"Nobody's eating anybody!" I yell, then burst into tears.

"OK," Dervish soothes me. "I was only trying to help. Don't worry. If you don't want to eat me, I won't force you." He pulls a crooked expression. "Did that sound as crazy as I think?"

I laugh through my tears. "You idiot! Besides," I add, wiping my cheeks clean, "it doesn't matter whether we live or die. It might even be better if we perish on this boat. I'm not sure I want to go back."

"What are you talking about?" Dervish frowns.

I take a deep breath and finally reveal what I learned on the ship. "I touched the Shadow and absorbed some of its memories. I told Beranabus. That's why he gambled so recklessly and sacrificed himself. He knew the Shadow couldn't be defeated, that we couldn't kill it. Sending it back to the Demonata universe for a while was the best we could hope for."

"I don't believe that," Dervish snorts. "I don't care how powerful it is. Everything can be killed."

"Not the Shadow," I disagree.

I lie back in the boat and stare at the darkening sky, listening to the waves lap against the sides of the boat. It's peaceful. I wouldn't mind if I fell asleep now and never awoke.

"The Shadow's not a demon," I explain quietly, and Dervish and Kirilli have to lean in close to hear. "It's a force that somehow acquired consciousness. I don't know how, but it has."

"A force?" Dervish scowls.

"Like gravity," I explain. "Imagine if gravity developed a mind, created a body, and became an actual entity — Gravity with a capital G, intelligent like us, able to think and plan."

"That's impossible," Dervish says. "Gravity's like the wind or sunlight. It can't develop consciousness."

"But imagine it could," I push. "You've seen the true nature of the universes. You know magic exists, that just about anything is possible. *Imagine.*"

Dervish takes a moment to adjust his thinking. "OK," he says heavily. "It's a struggle, but I'm running with it. Gravity has a mind. It's given itself a body. And it's coming after humanity. Is that what you're telling me?"

"Almost," I smile weakly. "But it's not gravity. It's an altogether different force. More sinister. Inescapable. Every living being's final companion."

"Don't tease us with riddles," Dervish snaps. "Just spit it out."

"I think I already know," Kirilli says softly. "The greatest stage magician ever was Harry Houdini. He was a master escapologist. He could cheat any trap known to man. But there was one thing he couldn't escape, no matter how hard he tried, and it caught him eventually — the Grim Reaper."

"Aye."

I sigh as Dervish stares at me with growing understanding and horror, then close my eyes and cross my hands over my chest. I think about Beranabus, Sharmila, Kernel. Dervish's weak heart. The trap Lord Loss set for Grubbs. What will happen to Kirilli and me if help doesn't arrive in time.

Dead ends everywhere. The dead coming back to life on the ship. Juni and I returning to life from beyond the grave. The Shadow's promise to the Demonata, that they'll live forever once the war with humanity is over.

"The Shadow is ancient beyond understanding," I whisper. "It's as old as life. It doesn't have an actual name. It never needed one. But we've given it a title. The demons have too. It's the darkness when a light is quenched, the silence when a sound fades. It takes the final breath from the smallest insect and the mightiest king. It knows us all, stalks us all, and in the end claims us all.

"The Shadow is *Death*."

The horrifying adventures continue in

WOLF ISLAND

Book 8 in THE DEMONATA series

Available now from Little, Brown and Company

Turn the page for a sneak peek. . . .

A FIVE-HEADED demon with the body of a giant earwig bears down on me. I leap high into the air and unleash a paralyzing spell. The demon stiffens, quivers wildly, then collapses. Its brittle legs shatter beneath the weight of its oversized body. Beranabus and Kernel move in on the helpless bug. I follow halfheartedly, stifling a yawn. Just another dull day at the office.

One of the demon's heads looks like a crow, another a vulture, while the rest look like nothing on Earth. It opens its birdlike beak and squirts a thick green liquid. Beranabus ducks swiftly, but the spit catches Kernel's right arm. His flesh bubbles away to the bone. Cursing with more irritation than pain, he uses magic to cleanse his flesh and repair the damage.

"We could do with a bit of help here," Kernel growls as I stroll after them.

"I doubt it," I grunt, but break into a jog, just in case the demon's tougher than we anticipated. Wouldn't want to let the team down.

The earwig unleashes another ball of spit at Beranabus. The elderly magician flicks a hand at the liquid, which rebounds over the demon's heads. It screams with shock and then agony. Kernel, back to full health, freezes the acidic spit before it fries the creature's brains. We want this ugly baby alive.

I leap onto the demon's back. Its shell is slimy beneath my bare feet. Stinks worse than a thousand sweaty armpits. But in this universe that doesn't even begin to approach the boundaries of disgusting. I confronted a demon made of vomit a few months ago. The only way to subdue it was to suck on the strands of puke and sap it of its strength. Yum!

This wasn't a career move. I didn't read a prospectus and go, "Hmm, drinking demon puke . . . I could do that!" Life just led me here. I'm a magician, and if you're born with a power like mine, you tend to get drawn into the war with the Demonata hordes. I fought my destiny for a long time, but now I grudgingly accept it and get on with the job at hand.

The earwig shudders, overcoming my paralyzing spell. It tries to buck me off, but I dig my toes in and drive a fist through the shell. I let magical warmth flood from my fingers. An electric shock crackles through the demon. It squeals, then collapses limply beneath me.

Beranabus and Kernel face the demon's vulture-like head and interrogate it. I stay perched on its back, hand immersed in its gooey flesh, green blood staining my forearm, nose crinkled against the stench.

"What is it?" Beranabus shouts, punching the twisted head, then grabbing the beak. "What's its real name? Where's it from? How powerful is it? What are its plans?" He releases his hold and waits for an answer.

The demon only moans in response. There are thousands of demon languages. I can't speak any, but there are spells you can cast to understand them. I generally don't bother. I'm sure this demon knows no more about the mysterious Shadow than any of the hundreds we've tormented over the last however many months that we've been on this wild goose chase.

The Shadow is the name we've given to a demon of immense power. It's a massive, pitch-black beast, seemingly stitched together out of patches of shadow, with hundreds of snakelike tentacles. Beranabus thinks it's the greatest threat we've ever faced. Lord Loss — an old foe of mine — said the Shadow was going to destroy the world. When a demon master makes a prediction like that, only a fool doesn't take note.

We've been searching for the monster ever since we first encountered it in a cave, on a night when I lost my brother, but saved the world. We've been trying to find out more about it by torturing creatures like this giant earwig. We know the Shadow has assembled an army of demons, promising them the destruction of mankind and even the end of death itself. But we don't know who it is, where it comes from, exactly how powerful it is.

"This is your last chance," Beranabus growls, taking a step back from the earwig. "Tell us what you know or we'll kill you."

The demon makes a series of spluttering noises. Beranabus and Kernel listen attentively while I scratch my neck and yawn again.

"The same old rubbish," Kernel murmurs when the demon finishes.

"Unless it's lying," Beranabus says without any real hope.

The earwig babbles rapidly, panicked.

"Spare you?" Beranabus muses, as if it's a novel idea. "Why should we?"

More squeaks and splutters.

"Very well," Beranabus says after a short pause. "But if you discover something and don't tell us . . ." There's no need for him to finish. The magician is feared in this universe of horrors. The earwig knows the many kinds of hell we could put it through.

I withdraw my hand from the hole in the earwig's shell and jump to the ground. We're in a gloomy realm, no sun in the dark purple sky. The land around us is like a desert. I make my hand hard and jab it into the dry earth, over and over, cleaning the green blood from my skin. Kernel opens a window while I'm doing that. When I'm ready, we step through into the next zone, in search of more demons to pump for information about the elusive, ominous Shadow.